THE GIRL
OF NEWGATE PRISON

THE GIRL
OF NEWGATE PRISON

DAVID STARR

RONSDALE PRESS

THE GIRL OF NEWGATE PRISON
Copyright © 2020 David Starr

RONSDALE PRESS
3350 West 21st Avenue, Vancouver, B.C. Canada V6S 1G7
www.ronsdalepress.com

Typesetting: Julie Cochrane, in Minion 12 pt on 16
Cover Art & Design: Nancy de Brouwer, Massive Graphic Design
Paper: 100 Edition, 55 lb. Antique Cream (FSC) — 100% post-consumer
    waste, totally chlorine-free and acid-free

Ronsdale Press wishes to thank the following for their support of its publishing program: the Canada Council for the Arts, the Government of Canada, the British Columbia Arts Council, and the Province of British Columbia through the British Columbia Book Publishing Tax Credit program.

Library and Archives Canada Cataloguing in Publication

Title: The girl of Newgate Prison / David Starr.
Names: Starr, David (School principal), author.
Description: Sequel to: The Nor'wester.
Identifiers: Canadiana (print) 20200286846 | Canadiana (ebook)
    20200286854 | ISBN 9781553806172 (softcover) | ISBN 9781553806189
    (ebook) | ISBN 9781553806196 (PDF)
Subjects: LCSH: Fry, Elizabeth Gurney, 1780–1845 — Juvenile fiction.
Classification: LCC PS8637.T365 G57 2020 | DDC jC813/.6–dc23

At Ronsdale Press we are committed to protecting the environment. To this end we are working with Canopy and printers to phase out our use of paper produced from ancient forests. This book is one step towards that goal.

Printed in Canada by Marquis Book Printing, Quebec

For Yvonne Starr:
It'll all work out

ACKNOWLEDGEMENTS

I would like to thank my wife Sharon and son Aidan for giving me the gift of time to write this story and others. I would also like to thank Ron and Veronica Hatch of Ronsdale Press for their support of Canadian writers telling stories that matter to Canadian readers. Thanks also to Hélène Leboucher, who prepared the novel for typesetting. Finally, I would like to thank Dusty, who has been waiting patiently for Libby to tell her story.

THE GIRL
OF NEWGATE PRISON

Chapter 1

LIVERPOOL — APRIL 1807

"THAT'S THE IRISH SEA you smell," Tinker says when we arrive at the docks. "Liverpool's one of the largest ports in England, and you'll see strange things here from all over the world. Mind you, keep your wits about you. There are plenty here who'd cut your purse or even your throat if they had the chance. People will do all sorts of bad things for a guinea or two."

People who would cut my throat. I squeeze the small bag of coins hidden in my jacket and cast my eyes nervously about. I've not told Tinker about the money and have told Duncan to do the same. I'm not sure why, exactly. Our travelling companion has been nothing but kind to us. Still, a feeling deep in my belly tells me to keep silent about it.

Tinker seems not to notice my discomfort as we walk along the docks until we arrive at a large, tin-roofed warehouse. "I have to meet me business associate here on the docks," he says as he enters the large open door.

"Go for a walk. I'm sure you'll find more interesting things on the waterfront than an old peddler replenishing his stock of pots and pans. But don't forget to keep your eyes open. Like I said, the docks ain't the safest place in Liverpool."

Dangerous or not, I am fascinated by the waterfront. The docks aren't on the open sea, not exactly, but rather they're built where the River Mersey empties into a bay. Ships of all sorts and sizes rest tied up, besides all manner of boxes, crates and other merchandise.

Everywhere we look men hurry about their tasks, clambering on and off the ships. One ship in particular catches my attention — and Duncan's as well, though not for anything good. A sick feeling rises in my stomach as I watch a wooden derrick lift a huge roll of cotton cloth from the dock and deposit it into a cargo hold. Perhaps I helped make that cloth. Perhaps that very roll is the last one my parents made before they burned to death in Hamilton's Cotton Mill in Glasgow.

I tear my eyes from the cloth and try to think of other things, so I look at the people milling about instead. Many are sailors and stevedores of all shapes, sizes and colours, but I also see people who are most definitely not workers. Men, women and children my age and younger lounge against piles of cargo and pilings. On one pitch-covered post, I see several posters, and I thank my mother that over my father's objections she'd taught me to read in the long, wet Highland winters. "*Come to America,*" "*New Orleans,*" and "*Halifax,*" the advertisements say.

I watch as Duncan approaches a boy about my own age, sitting on a crate. "Where are ye going?" Duncan asks.

"Boston," the boy replies with a Highland lilt of his own. Who knows? This lad could have been from Loch Tay, or any other small village in the north of Scotland for that matter.

He gestures at the *Leopard*, a small three-masted ship berthed at the end of the wharf. "Ma says in America there's land and food fer everybody and that we're gonna be rich."

His words strike a chord with Duncan; that is easy enough to tell by the smile on his face. "Libby, 'tis our chance! Let's go with them!" he whispers excitedly to me.

To leave Scotland is one thing; to climb on board a ship and cross the Atlantic Ocean is something altogether different. "I dinnae ken, Duncan," I reply nervously, my answer not the response he had been hoping for, by the sour look on his face.

"Why not? Would ye rather stay here with the army chasing us?"

Duncan has a point. I remember the soldiers with guns looking for us back in Glasgow before we fled. Maybe leaving Britain altogether is the safest thing to do. "Let's talk to Tinker and see what he has to say." The old man knows the docks.

Hopefully he knows something about the trip to America as well. "Besides, passage isn't free, remember? We have some money but I've no idea if it's enough."

Duncan agrees, though I know my rash brother would just as soon climb on board the *Leopard* right now. We turn around and try to find our way back to Tinker. We've wandered a great distance and have taken several wrong turns amongst the maze of ships and warehouses before we find our way back to where our friend conducts his business. I wait outside the warehouse, next to Tinker's pony and cart as Duncan walks inside. "Tinker!" I hear him call. "We need to talk to you."

In the shadows of the warehouse I see two shapes in silhouette. One of them is Tinker I can tell, the other, a tall man with a hat that looks somewhat familiar, though I can't tell for certain as he retreats into the darkness as Duncan approaches.

"What is it, lad?" Tinker says. "We ain't quite done our business yet."

"I have something very important to ask ye about." I hear my brother say.

"Wait outside for me by the cart and I'll join you presently," says Tinker.

Duncan steps impatiently out of the warehouse and comes back to me. He sits on the back of the cart while I scratch the pony's ears. As we wait, an old sailor sitting under a blanket against the side of the warehouse catches my eye.

"Can thou spare a copper for a wounded veteran of His Majesty's Navy? Name's John. I was on the *Captain* with Admiral Nelson at the battle of Cape St. Vincent. We gave the Spaniards a sound thrashing that day, but I didn't escape unscathed."

John lifts the blanket. I gasp when I see both his legs have been amputated below his knees. "His Majesty's Navy has no use for a cripple, even a war hero, and I've been here on the docks ever since, begging kind lasses like thyself for a few coppers to buy bread."

I place a penny into John's outstretched hand. "Here ye go, ye poor man." It isn't much, though Duncan is not happy at my decision.

"Libby! We need all our money to sail to America!"

"A penny won't buy us passage, Duncan, but it will feed this man fer a day or two." I am angry that my brother is so without compassion he would deny the old sailor a small copper coin.

John places the penny inside his tattered coat. "God bless you, miss, thy generosity won't be forgotten. But you, young man, could learn a thing or two about kindness. Someday thine own life might hang in the balance. When it does, I hope you meet people more charitable than thyself."

The sailor takes his leave and shuffles away on his stumps. "I bet he's going to spend that coin on drink," Duncan says looking most unhappy, not pleased to be lectured by the old man — or me.

"And what if he does? It was the least we could do." That silences my brother. I may be younger, but I've not lost an argument with Duncan in my entire life. Duncan knows there is nothing to gain by carrying on, and so he ignores me until Tinker's tiny frame appears in the door of the warehouse.

"So what bee's gotten into your bonnet?"

Duncan is hardly able to contain his excitement. "There's a ship on the docks taking people to Boston, and we want to sail on it."

"Boston." Tinker has a strange look in his eyes as he speaks. "Do you even know where Boston is, lad?"

Duncan points over the docks towards the open sea. "That way?"

Tinker looks westward. "It is, but you have to survive crossing the ocean to get there. Many ships leave this port, and ain't never seen again. They just disappear, swallowed up whole by the storms. There are waves a hundred feet high out there, you know. Untold thousands have died on the Atlantic. There ain't nothing wrong with taking great risks but know what you're getting yourself in for."

A seagull flies amongst the masts. Tinker watches in silence for a while until the bird disappears. "A part of me would like to go as well. I thought about it once, but I was never brave, and I'm too old for such travels now. Ain't much use for anything really," he says, in an odd tone. "Not no more."

"Do ye have any idea how much it would cost to travel to Boston?" Duncan asks.

"How much money do you have?" Duncan looks at me with desperate eyes. I know exactly what he wants me to do and so reluctantly I show Tinker the sack we took from our old place in Glasgow. He takes the bag, has a quick look inside, then gives it back to me, though for a moment I'm not sure if he isn't going to slip it inside his own coat.

Tinker shakes his head sadly. "Ain't enough by far. You'll both need to work for a year or two, but if you save your wages you can be on your way before you know it."

"A year?" Duncan cries. "We have to wait a whole year?"

Tinker's eyes flit back into the dark warehouse. I don't know what exactly, but something about him seems very strange right now. "Why don't I go and talk to my friend about a job for you?" he suggests. "They're always looking for strong backs on the waterfront. What do you think?"

"Thank ye, Tinker, that would be appreciated," I say, though the last thing I want is to work on the docks. Save for the fresh air, they don't seem much different from the mill to me.

"Wait here then," the peddler tells us. "I'll have a quick word and I'll be right back."

Duncan can hardly stand waiting. He sits back on the cart, nearly bouncing with excitement. I turn my attention to the pony. I scratch his ears once more, wishing I had a carrot to feed him. I am lost in my own thoughts, thinking about sailing to America and trying to understand just why I feel so uneasy when Duncan speaks.

"Libby." His tone is quiet, but I know my brother better

than any person alive, and I can hear the fright in his voice. I hurry to him, watching as he lifts a shaking hand. Clenched in his fingers is a piece of paper he has found in the cart. A poster, I can see, a poster with the date, Duncan's name and a very recognizable drawing of his face.

"*Wanted for Attempted Murder,*" it reads, "*Sixteen-year-old Duncan Scott, recently of Glasgow. Five guinea reward if alive, three guineas dead. The fugitive is believed to have entered England in April 1807, likely in the company of Elizabeth Scott, his fourteen-year-old sister.*"

Chapter 2

"HOW COULD HE HAVE known about . . ." Something moves in the warehouse. In shock at what I see approaching, I clamp my hand tightly over Duncan's mouth and pull him away from the cart, towards a large stack of crates. We need to be silent right now, invisible. My eyes bright with fright, I point to the door.

Tinker emerges from the shadows, dwarfed alongside a large man in an English army uniform. I knew I recognized the man's hat; it was the very same kind the soldiers who beat up Angus wore. The soldier holds a copy of the wanted poster in his hands, the same as the one Duncan found in the cart. "The boy told me his name was Angus, Major," Tinker says, "but that's definitely 'im."

Tinker coughs gently and lifts his hand expectantly. "The reward? Five guineas if captured alive, it said? I saw the poster in Carlisle a week ago, could have slit both their throats while they slept to collect the easy three, but I didn't. I'm kind, I am."

The major drops a gold coin into Tinker's outstretched hand. "You are a very compassionate man, indeed," he says, though by the tone in his voice I know the soldier means something else entirely. "There's one guinea now. You'll get the rest when my men have the boy in irons. Where is he?"

Tinker waves towards the docks. "Just over there. I told 'im to wait by the cart. Went for a walk probably. They don't suspect a thing; they think I'm their friend."

Despite my own warning to be silent, I nearly cry in horror when a pack of armed soldiers, a dozen at least, come out of the gloom of the warehouse and stand beside their commanding officer. "We'll find him," the major says as the men assemble, waiting orders. "That scum nearly killed a nobleman and he'll soon have his neck stretched for it."

Duncan is frozen, much like he was back in our old tenement in Glasgow after he attacked Cecil Hamilton for hurting me. He needs my help, I know it. If I don't do something the soldiers will find us and my brother will hang. I grasp Duncan's hand and gently pull him away from the crates, edging our way slowly down the dock, staying low and out of sight, praying we aren't noticed.

We round the corner and run as fast as we can. "How

could Tinker do this to us?" Duncan asks, heartbreak in his voice.

How? For five gold guineas. That was what the poster said and that is what Tinker asked for. Now let's find that ship."

"But we dinnae have enough money! We need to pay for passage, remember?"

"And ye believe Tinker after what he tried to do?" I reply breathlessly as we hurry along the waterfront back towards the *Leopard*. "He'd have said anything to stop us from leaving so he could collect the reward."

In truth I have no idea how much money we need for passage across the Atlantic, to Boston or New York or any other place. I just hope that our few coins will suffice and that we will soon be sailing away from Liverpool, leaving our treasonous travelling companion, the soldiers and Sir Cecil Hamilton far behind in our wake.

We reach the *Leopard*'s berth and when we do I nearly cry. The *Leopard* has already pulled away from the dock, and though the ship is only one hundred yards out of port it may as well be a million miles away. Suddenly a loud commotion rises behind us. "In the name of King George, get out of our way!" cries a soldier. Panicked, I look along the docks. There is another ship, the *Sylph*, tied up alongside the dock, not ten yards away. Its gangplank is extended and unguarded.

"Duncan! Get on that ship this moment and hide! I'll wait here and distract them! It's not me they're after, and if yer caught ye'll die!"

Duncan will have none of it. "Libby! Come with me! The soldiers are almost here!"

"Are ye mad? If I do, they'll climb on board, tear this ship apart and find the both of us." I take his hand and drag my brother to the gangplank. "No matter what happens, stay hidden until they go. I'll be fine. They'll probably just ask some questions, then let me go. I'll get ye when it's safe. Just don't move until I come. Promise me ye won't."

"I can't leave ye!" Even with his very life at risk, Duncan is obstinate. He will not abandon me.

"Get on that ship this instant, Duncan!" It tears my heart in two to be separated from the only family I have left, but if he doesn't get away he will swing from a Glasgow gallows. That I cannot allow.

"They must be down here!" a soldier yells. "We 'ave 'em now!"

Duncan knows I am right, that he has no other choice. He slowly, reluctantly steps towards the gangplank. "I love ye, Libby."

I take our small bag of coins and give it to Duncan. "I love ye, too, Duncan. Just promise me ye'll stay hidden no matter what."

"I will," Duncan says as he runs quickly up the gangplank. From the dock I watch anxiously. Neither one of us has ever been on a ship before. Duncan has no idea where to go on board, I can tell, and my heart races as I watch him looking frantically for a safe place to hide.

Finally, Duncan climbs under the canvas cover of a small boat on the ship's deck. I watch as he lifts the tarp, crawls into the boat and vanishes from my sight.

"There's the girl!" a soldier cries as the sound of the boots quicken along the wooden dock. They quickly reach me, and two strong soldiers grab my arms so I cannot run away — as if there was any place to go. "You! Missy! Where's your brother?"

I look to the *Leopard*, free and clear of the docks, making her way for open water. "On that ship."

"Damnation! He's 'alf a mile out to sea!" the soldier says. The plan that came to me is very simple. We may not have been able to sail on the *Leopard*, but the ship can still help us as a decoy. I feel the faintest flicker of hope. Duncan and I may just get out of this after all.

"Shall we get the navy?" another soldier asks.

"Don't be daft. The Royal Navy won't mobilize for a mere boy, no matter who he beat 'alf to death!"

The major, the man who gave Tinker his blood money, catches up to his troops. "You think your brother has escaped justice do you, young lady?" he asks me.

"Defending yer family is not a crime, my laird," I say. I'm scared out of my skin, but I'll not let these men know it.

"It is when the man he attacks is a friend of the King. Search the other vessel," the major orders. "This could be some sort of a trick."

My heart is in my throat as I watch two soldiers walk up

the gangplank of the *Sylph*. "Waste of time, this," I hear one of the soldiers say. "The brat's a league out to sea, laughing at us. A bit of a coward though, don't you think? To abandon his sister like that? What sort of villain could he be?"

"A terrible coward indeed," says the other. "You're probably right, he's on the other ship, no doubt, but you know the army same as me; do as you're told or else. Let's 'ave a quick look and get this over with."

Coward. The word angers me so much I want to hit the soldier who said it. Duncan is the bravest person I know. He stood up for me when Sir Cecil Hamilton hit me and he put his own life at risk to save mine. He is the farthest thing from a coward.

"You there!" I hear a voice rise from on board the *Sylph*. "What are you doing on my ship?"

"Searching for a wanted criminal. What's it to you?"

"I'm the captain of this vessel." A stern-looking man with a white beard appears at the side of the ship. "People boarding her need my permission, even soldiers of the realm."

"Sorry, sir," the soldier says, deferring to rank by the sound of the man's voice. On land or at sea, a captain is superior to a regular soldier. "Orders. We're looking for a terrible criminal who fled the King's justice."

The captain laughs at that comment. "King's justice? The wretch probably stole a carrot from some duke's kitchen."

No! I want to shout. *He saved my life from a thug with a noble title. He's no thief! He's a hero!*

"Oh no, sir! I ain't sure exactly what he done but there's a five-guinea reward on his head. Murdered a lord or something by the sounds of it."

"In that case be quick about it," the captain says, though I can tell he is little pleased to have the soldiers on his ship. "We sail on the next tide and you two don't look like the type who'd fancy a trip across the Atlantic this time of year."

I watch as the solders check hatchways and doors. "Everything's locked up tight," one says. "Let's just 'ave a look in that small boat over there so we can tell the Major we did our jobs proper."

I want to shout a warning to Duncan as they near the boat, but I know if I do I will give up my brother's hiding place and he will be caught for sure. Instead I watch, praying silently for a miracle.

One of the soldiers pulls back the canvas cover at one end of the boat. I can't breathe, certain Duncan will be found. I wait for what seems to be an eternity, then stifle a relieved gasp as the soldier walks away — without my brother in custody.

"He ain't aboard, sir," he says to their major as the two of them leave the ship and walk down the gangplank to the docks. "The brat must be on the other ship — just like the girl said."

"I told ye," I say to the officer. "Now ye can let me go and be on yer way."

"Oh, I don't think so, lass," the Major replies. He looks at one of his men who produces a set of heavy irons and quickly locks up my wrists. "You're coming with us."

"But I haven't done anything wrong!"

I fight the rising horror in my chest. This is not part of the plan. Despite myself, I look to the small canvas-covered boat on the deck, hoping against hope that Duncan will stay hidden and not try some fool-hardy attempt to rescue me. At best he'll be captured and hung. At worst? A bullet or a sword will kill him here and now.

Just don't move until I come. That was what I told him. For his sake I pray Duncan heeds my words and doesn't do anything foolish.

"Wanted or not, you can explain things to Colonel Phillips yourself, young lady," the major says. "He'll be most displeased with this turn of events and will want to hear about it from you personally. Someone has to pay for your brother's crimes, and it seems that person is you."

Chapter 3

⚬

NOW WHAT? THE MAJOR'S troop of Redcoats surround me, armed with rifles, pistols and long swords. I could slip my chains and run. *Someone must pay for your brother's crimes, and it seems that person is you.* The major's words send cold chills right through me. At first, I thought I would merely be questioned. Duncan was the one they wanted, not me. The reward of five gold guineas was on his head, not mine. I had assumed I was safe. Now I know that I am not.

Duncan would have paid with his life had he been caught. A rough rope noose would have been placed around his neck and he would have dropped to his death. Is that what they mean to do to me since they don't have him? My hands shake and my heart races. I will not let that happen. I know for certain that I must escape. Even a bullet in the back as I flee would be a better death than hanging.

"You're gonna wish your brother hadn't flown the coop, missy!" a soldier to my right tells me, as if I needed any more proof of their intent. I am at the front of the procession. Two soldiers march beside me, one on either side. They assume they have me, that the irons around my wrists are enough.

If I were a man, or even a boy like my brother, there would be chains around my legs. Perhaps I would have been manacled to the wrist of a soldier as well, but they have not taken those precautions. I am just a wee girl after all, and I will use their arrogance to my benefit.

I wait patiently for my chance, listening to the sound of boots clumping around me on the wooden docks, the chatter of the soldiers as we march. I look at the faces of the stevedores, sailors and migrants as we go. Most turn their heads away, afraid to make eye contact with the soldiers. In the few faces that do look at me, I see pity. That and anger at the sight of a young girl in the clutches of the army. The Redcoats have few friends here, I can tell.

The soldiers gossip as we walk. "So, I tells the sergeant it just ain't fair," complains one to my right, a short pudgy man with bad skin. "I dunged out the barracks stables three times this week already. It's Wilson's turn, I told him. He ain't done it once, yet."

"How'd that work out for you, mate?"

"About as well as you'd think. Wilson's the sergeant's pet after all. I still had to clean the stables, then I got extra sentry duty for my troubles. The army, mate. I tell you . . ."

The men pay no attention to me whatsoever, absorbed as they are in their griping. This is my opportunity. I look about the docks, to the warren of walkways, warehouses and ships spread out before me. I am fast, after all. I used to run like a rabbit in the fields around Loch Tay and nobody could catch me, not even Duncan. All I need to do is slip these chains, run and pray there are places to hide on the waterfront.

I gather both my breath and my courage. I cast a glimpse at the soldier on either side of me. They are still gossiping about one thing or the other. Slowly I move my left hand to my right wrist. I work the manacle, carefully, ever so carefully twisting and pulling, the metal scraping and pinching on my skin. As I pull my knuckles through, I make a fist to keep it from falling off before I am ready to make my escape.

I repeat the process with my right hand, gently tugging the iron circlet down over my left wrist, until it, too, has slipped over the bones. I breathe, working up the courage to run. When I do, I know that I must be as quick as a deer chased by wolves. After all, my life depends on it.

This time it won't be my brother or one of my old friends coming after me in a game of chase. It will be Redcoats with swords and guns. If I am caught? I put the thought away, take one last breath, steel my nerves. One way or another, I won't let them hang me.

Chapter 4

 ∽

"OI! WHAT THE BLAZES?" The shout comes from behind me when I slip off the manacles and dash away.

"Stop or I'll shoot!" says another, but I don't stop. Instead, I wheel around a stack of wooden crates, running down a wooden walkway as quickly as I can. A gun erupts, the sharp crack of the rifle nearly deafening me. Two other shots ring out, one after the other.

Above my head, not more than half a foot, I feel a rush of air as a musket ball passes over me and slams into a tarred piling. "Hold your fire, you idiots!" the major yells. "Colonel Phillips will want her alive!" The guns fall silent, replaced by a stampede of heavy boots as the soldiers follow along in my wake. I don't know who this Colonel Phillips is, and I care not to find out. He can't want me for anything good.

I run faster, faster than ever before, my heart pounding, blood throbbing in my ears. Around me dockworkers watch as I sprint past them, not helping but not hindering my escape either. My eyes dart everywhere, looking for a place to hide, a place to run.

Ahead is a large warehouse, doors open. I rush through them and into the cavernous building. The warehouse is full of chests, crates and sea chests, goods from across Britain, from across the world, no doubt. If I had time I could pop the lid from one of them, crawl inside, bury deep underneath whatever cargo it holds and hide, but the Redcoats are already in the warehouse. They can see me, would know in a heartbeat where I was. I must run instead.

I am almost through the building when another large door beckons ahead, the thin shape of a mast dead ahead. I race towards the door, then through it full tilt, back onto the docks.

"Run girl! Don't let them get you!" John, the same legless sailor I gave a penny to not an hour ago, watches me from against a piling, urging me on. I have no time to say anything. Instead, I just watch John drag himself out into the middle of the dock as I pass.

"Get out of the way, you old cripple!"

Though I can't see him, I know that the dear man is trying his best to block the charging Redcoats, to slow them down,

Chapter 5

THE WATER TEARS my breath from my lungs. It is cold, far colder than I could have possibly imagined, and it has me in its grasp. The weight of my skirts and shoes are pulling me down, slowly, unstoppably into its murky, oily depths. I panic, feet kicking madly, hands flailing wildly as I fight to stop my descent. Though my eyes are open, I can scarce see more than a foot in front of my face. The weight of the water presses down upon me, holding me in its grasp.

Suddenly my left hand hits a piling. I try desperately to hold onto the wood, to pull myself up to the surface, but it is slimy and slippery, my efforts futile. It is then I realize that I may never feel the heat of the sun on my face again, never breathe in clear mountain air again, nor ever see my brother again. My chest feels as if it will explode, I start to faint. I close my eyes. I am about to die and know it.

Then my fingers brush up against something else. Something metal, something I can grab. I open my eyes and through the murky water I see the weed-covered rung of a metal ladder, a ladder attached to a piling, a ladder that leads up to the surface of the bay.

With my remaining strength I climb, one rung at a time. The light from above grows brighter and brighter as I inch my way up, out of the water of Liverpool Bay. I feel my hand break the surface. Then, with one last frantic lunge, my face emerges. I gasp, gulping in the air.

"Damnation! Does anyone see her?"

I hear a voice. I look up, trying not to cough, not to gag and draw attention to my location. I have drifted back towards the main wharves, some thirty feet from where I jumped in. All the soldiers are staring into the water, their backs towards me, but all it would take is one to turn around and I would be seen.

I reach under the dock to a barnacle-covered beam. I pull myself along the wood, and though my hands start to bleed, cut by the sharp edges of the shells, I move until I am deep under the dock and out of sight. Hands aching, I hold on, listening to the soldiers talk.

"Come on then, men. There's no point in us standing here any longer. She's drowned for sure, dead at the bottom of the bay. We need to return to barracks and report to Colonel Phillips. I cannot imagine he will be pleased with this news."

The major sounds most disappointed as he trudges away, the rest of his men following behind. The soldiers walk until they are right above me, their boots dislodging dirt and dust that falls like brown snow onto the water. They do not stop. As far as the British Army is concerned, I am dead.

I'm shivering wildly. The water is cold, and though the April sun holds little warmth, I know I need to climb out from under the dock and dry off. As hard as it is to wait, however, I give the Redcoats and whatever audience has gathered, another five minutes to disperse until I dare to edge my way back to the ladder.

With my entire body shaking and my hands throbbing and bleeding, I slowly pull myself up the ladder. I peer cautiously over the edge of the wooden decking but see no one about. Slowly, one hand, one foot at a time, I climb until I collapse on the dock. I can hardly breathe for the cold, can hardly feel my hands anymore as the chill sets in as I lie there, under the pale spring sun.

"That was a neat trick, lass." I turn my head to see John, the crippled sailor leaning against a crate. "I'm glad to see thou art still alive."

"Ye tried to stop them," I gasp, remembering how John put himself between me and the charging soldiers.

John shuffles towards me as he speaks. "Aye, though I failed in that regard. Thou were very brave to jump into the water like that. I was certain the cold and the currents took you."

"For a moment I thought they did as well."

I see a nervous look in John's eyes. "Thou still ain't safe, though. We need to get thee hidden before any of these wharf rats tell the army thou still breathe. That and we need to get thee warm and dry before the cold does the army's dirty work. Can thou walk?"

It is sheer agony to pull myself to my feet, but somehow I do, much to the approval of the sailor. "Aye. Barely."

"Good," he beams. "Follow me. I know a nice spot where thou'll be safe."

Chapter 6

"NOT QUITE WINDSOR CASTLE but it serves well enough. Welcome to my home."

John's home, such as it is, is a collection of large, empty crates behind what looks to be an abandoned warehouse just a few minutes walk from where I jumped into Liverpool Bay.

A fire burns in a small metal barrel covered by a grate. Beside it, stand two other men, both looking at me curiously. "Lads, say hello to my friend. Libby, isn't it?" John asks. "I think that's what thy brother called thee."

"Aye. Libby it is. A pleasure to meet ye."

"Name's Adam," says a thin old man with a long white beard and a friendly smile.

"Will." Will is younger than John, short and heavy-set with a clean-shaven face and black hair.

"Come on, then, young Libby," John says. "Sit thyself by the fire and get warm while I make a nice cup of tea." I do as John says and nearly cry in relief when I feel the heat of the flames on my face.

John reaches into a crate and gives me a thick woolen blanket that I quickly wrap myself in. While I dry off, John puts a metal pot full of water on the grate. Within a few short minutes the water is bubbling furiously. He drops a handful of tea into the water, fetches a pewter mug, strains the tea and passes the mug over to me. "I put some sugar in the cup as well," he says as I take a drink of the hot, sweet tea. "A well-deserved treat after your day."

Never in all my life have I tasted anything so delicious. "Thank ye," I say gratefully. "How did ye manage to get tea and sugar down here?"

Adam grins, a smile that shows more holes in his gums than teeth. "These are the docks, dearie. Stuff from around the world comes here. Sometimes some of it falls out of a crate or a sack and gets left behind. We find some of these things and put them to good use. Waste not, want not; that's what I say."

"And sometimes we help things *fall* from the crates and the sacks ourselves, if you know what I mean," adds Will with a mischievous grin. "A ship may have two tons of sugar from Jamaica when it arrives. Who will miss a few small pounds out of all that?"

"A man must survive," John says apologetically. "All three of us are veterans of the Royal Navy and suffered grievous wounds in defence of our country. We don't consider it stealing, so much as collecting a small pension for our service."

It is then I see what John is talking about. Adam is missing his right arm below the elbow and Will's left leg below the knee is gone. "Yes," Will agrees. "We all deserve a little recompense for our sacrifices in the name of King and country."

"So, what am I going to do now?" I ask myself. The fire is warm, and my clothes have started to dry, but my hands feel as if they are on fire from the sharp barnacles, and while I am safe for the time being, I have no idea what to do next.

Will takes a crutch and hops over to a chest. "Now you eat and get some rest." My heart nearly stops when I see a loaf of bread and a large chunk of cheese emerge from the chest.

"Eat as much as you want," he says making his way to me, the food in his free hand. There's more where that came from if thou need it. As Adam said: the Liverpool docks are full of all manner of things."

I'm soon feeling much better. The food and the fire have done wonders for me, and I am getting drowsy, but I must find a way to get to Duncan. "The ships that leave Liverpool," I ask. Do they go straight to America?"

Old Adam pipes up. "*Leopard*'s a migrant ship, lass. Liverpool's her home base but she'll be stopping in Dublin to pick up more passengers on her way to America. She'll stay in port in Ireland at least a few days while she loads her cargo and provisions. No doubt your brother will wait with it."

"Do all the migrant ships stop in Dublin," I ask. It is the *Sylph* I am worried about, though I cannot tell my friends the truth.

"Aye, most that sail from Liverpool, anyway," Adam says. "Next to cloth, the Irish are our biggest export these days."

"Funny thou should ask," John said. "Another ship left yesterday, not long after the *Leopard*. The *Sylph* her name is. She's on her way to Canada, Quebec to be specific."

My heart skips a beat. So that is where the *Sylph* is sailing! Now I know where my brother is bound for, perhaps I can find my own way there. But then my excitement is quickly replaced by panic. Surely John doesn't know the truth about Duncan? If he does, my brother's safety is in jeopardy. "I dinnae ken what thats got to do with me," I say as casually as I can.

A large knowing smile creases John's face. "Oh, nothing I'm sure. But if it did interest thee, the *Sylph* is stopping in Dublin as well. And do thou know what else is interesting?" John asks.

"I cannae imagine. What?"

"I happen to know the bosun of the *Elsa*. That's another migrant ship docked just down the way. He's a mate from my navy days. *Elsa's* sailing to New York at dawn, but she'll be stopping in Dublin as well. Might be that I could ask him to take thee along, as a favour for me. No doubt thou could find thy brother there. Is that interesting enough for thee?"

I cannae help crying. "Thank ye so much!" I say. I get up and hug the old man tightly. John saved my life by getting me warm and hiding me. For that alone I am grateful beyond words, but to help me get to Duncan? I owe him a debt I can never repay.

"Easy, girl," he says, blushing. "I'm just repaying the kindness thou showed me." Overhead the sky darkens. "Time to get some sleep. It's gonna be a busy day tomorrow. Take my bed," he says, pointing towards one of the wooden crates. "It ain't exactly a goose down mattress, but thou'll be warm enough. I'll bunk in with Adam tonight. Rest well, young Libby. With a bit of luck, thou will find thy brother soon."

Chapter 7

"TIME TO GO, LASS."

"Go?" Confused, I open my eyes, and through the gloom I see John, the crippled sailor, leaning over me. It is then I remember the events of yesterday: Duncan's escape on the *Sylph*, my capture and escape from the Redcoats, my desperate jump into Liverpool Bay, and John helping me after I crawled out of the water, cold and bleeding.

My hands feel slightly better this morning. They still ache but the pain from the shell cuts has dulled somewhat. Maybe they are healing or maybe I just don't notice the pain because I know in very short order I will be on a ship bound for Dublin — and Duncan.

Chapter 8

᷑

MY HEART NEAR BURSTS *when I see Duncan walking down the dock. His face, a young reflection of our late father's, breaks out into a wide grin when he sees me. "I never thought I'd see ye again, Libby," he weeps, catching me up in an embrace.*

"Nor I ye," I cry, my own tears streaming down my cheeks.

"Is this real and not some dream?" I ask, not daring to believe it.

"Aye," says Duncan, reluctantly breaking our hug. "Naught could keep me away, Libby. Ye are my family, after all. We've a new home, far from this place where we'll be safe, never bothered by the English again."

"We're leaving? Now?" I dare not believe the news.

"Aye, Libby, we are. With them." I look down the water-front. Behind Duncan is a ship, her crew standing expectantly on her deck.

"The cap'n is a friend of mine. He's taking on a load of cloth to Canada and we will be sailing with him on the evening tide, so gather your things, little sister, 'tis time to go."

"Get up, missy! It's time to go!" A harsh voice cries as Duncan, the dock and the waiting ship behind him disappear, replaced by a sharp pain in my side and the ugly face of an English soldier staring down at me.

I wake up on the cold floor of my cell. There is no bed in this place and since I arrived here, goodness knows how many days ago now, I've been sleeping on a pile of mouldy hay on the stones. I start to my feet but am moving too slowly for my gaoler's liking. "I said it's time to go!" he bellows, tapping me smartly with his toe. "Now get up, or I'll kick you again, understand?"

I stand unsteadily as he places my hands and ankles in heavy iron manacles then marches me out of the cell, up a flight of stone stairs to a large office. The soldier sits me down roughly in a wooden chair in front of a large desk. "Colonel Phillips wants a word with you, so no funny stuff like you pulled on the docks, understand?"

"Aye, my laird."

I have neither the plan nor the ability for *funny stuff*, what with the heavy iron circlets locked tightly on my wrists and ankles this time, and the soldier with the rifle and the heavy boots standing next me.

Light floods in through the window. Its early morning, I reckon, judging by the sun visible through the window, and I wait in silence for what seems hours, until I hear heavy footsteps outside in the hallway.

I draw in my breath anxiously as the door squeaks open and an officer, Colonel Phillips, I wager, heavy-set and brutish-looking, walks into the office. He sits in the comfortable, padded seat behind the desk, then pours himself a drink from a crystal decanter. It is only after he has downed the drink that he turns to me.

Another soldier enters the office with a book and a quill; he sits patiently at a small table beside the colonel. Pen in hand, waiting.

"Well then," Colonel Phillips sniffs. "So this is Elizabeth Scott, the Highland wench who led half of the King's Regiment of Foot — my regiment, I'll have you know — on a merry chase along the waterfront. I'm sorry to be the one to tell you this, but you are in a most precarious position, indeed."

"My laird," I say respectfully. "I dinnae ken why ye've locked me up. I've done naught wrong."

The English army officer is round, sweaty and balding, but what he is not, as far as I can tell, is one bit sorry about my position, or anything else about me. Without warning, Colonel Phillips draws back his hand, leans over the desk, and slaps me hard across my face, nearly knocking me from the chair.

I cry out from the pain, and the shock of the hit, my ears ringing, cheek burning as if it were on fire. "I would have thought a few days alone in the cells to think about things would make you realize the gravity of your situation, but I see the time was wasted on you."

Colonel Phillips' face is flushed as he pours himself another drink, then sits back down, draining the glass in one deep swig. *Nothing wrong?*" he wheezes once more, ignoring my sobs as he wipes his lips with the back of his sleeve.

"*Nothing wrong?* How about lying to an officer of the British Army? How about impugning the reputation of a member of the House of Lords and nearly killing him? How about fleeing the King's justice? Do you deny these charges?"

"My laird," I say softly, fearful of another hit. "I have told yer men the truth."

"Rubbish! You really expect me to believe you when you say that right after your parents died in a fire at the cotton mill in Glasgow, Sir Cecil rides up to see his business in flames and then, for no reason at all, he strikes *you*, of all people, knocking you to the ground."

"But he did, sir," I say, tears flowing from my eyes.

"And you also dare claim that your brother isn't a murderous wretch? That he didn't beat a nobleman half to death? Do you really expect me to believe that?"

Colonel Phillips pours himself a third drink and turns his attention to the soldier in the room, the one with the quill. "Taylor, make sure you write this down accurately, the information will be needed later for her trial."

"My laird," I stutter in response. The quill scratches across the paper. "'Tis true, I swear it, every word. My brother was provoked. All he did was defend me."

The English officer clearly does not believe me. "It was attempted murder. Both the reward on his head and the noose waiting for his inevitable capture are completely justifiable for his outrageous crimes."

"My laird," I beg. "Please, I cannae tell you how sorry I am about what happened, but we'd just lost our parents and Sir Cecil struck me with his cane. It was a rash act, I ken, but my brother lost his head just for a moment." Colonel Phillips pours himself another drink, his fourth in our short time together.

"But somehow, he found his head quickly enough to travel under an assumed name, cross the border and try to leave England entirely? That sounds more calculated than confused to me. Thank goodness that travelling pedlar recognized you. What was his name again? I read it in the report, but it escapes me. Tim, Tiny? It was something like that, I believe. Without him and that one-legged fellow on the docks you would never have gotten away with it."

"Tinker. His name was Tinker."

I hate the memory of that treacherous little viper, a man I thought was my true friend.

"Ah yes," the colonel says, "Tinker. But then your brother proved his cowardice once again by leaving you to face justice alone on the Liverpool waterfront, while he escaped to

Boston. He'll be caught sooner or later, make no mistake about it, just as you were. Thought you had escaped as well, didn't you? I can't imagine what is going through your pathetic head right now."

Not that I would ever tell this pig of a man, but my only thought is that Duncan is free, though where he is I do not know. Is he in Ireland trying to find passage back to me or is he on his way to Quebec?

Colonel Phillips is oblivious to the turmoil in my mind. "And now you are here — at least for the present. How have you found your accommodations? They're not the finest in Liverpool, I know, but you Scots are used to roughing it, unless I'm very much mistaken."

"They've been fine, thank ye." I've eaten nothing but stale bread, drunk nothing but water, slept on old straw and am terrified, if truth be told, but I'm not about to give this man the satisfaction of knowing how I truly feel. After all, he has been wrong about many things, has Colonel Phillips, but of one thing the English officer is right enough. My position does seem precarious. "What is to happen to me, then?"

"*What will happen to you?*" he repeats my question slowly, rolling each word around in his mouth. "I am a simple soldier, not a lawyer and the intricacies of the law are far beyond me, but it's my understanding you're to be charged for the attempted murder of Sir Cecil Hamilton, for aiding a felon to escape, for slander and for fleeing from the King's justice yourself. These are most serious crimes. Capital crimes.

Justice demands that someone dangle from the gibbet because of them, and that someone is you."

Colonel Phillips motions at the soldier who brought me out of the cell. He hurries over and pulls me roughly out of the chair.

"Your brother may have escaped justice, but you won't. If it were up to me, I'd have you hanged in the regimental square today, but higher ranks than I have decided your fate. There's a spot reserved for you at Newgate. You're leaving for London immediately. Enjoy the trip south; it will be the last time you breathe free air again."

Chapter 9

ঔ০

I'M THE ONLY PASSENGER in the prison wagon, and for twelve long hours I sit alone on a hard, wooden bench, my wrists and ankles in shackles as we bounce over the rough road. A soldier, an older-looking man, drives the heavy cart. We stop just twice to rest and water the two horses that pull us along. He doesn't speak to me at all, the soldier, nor does he offer me any food or water.

The large metal bars on the door give me a view of the countryside, but they also allow passersby to see me. Most are not kind. In the Northern England town of Chester, a group of lads, several years younger than me, follow the wagon, tormenting me. "You're gonna hang, you witch!" they jeer and hoot, throwing rocks at the bars until the soldier shoos them away.

This scene is repeated in several other villages we pass through: young men targeting the wagon with hateful words, rocks and rotten vegetables. Even if I'd been left alone by the people we pass, the trip is torture. Within hours after leaving Liverpool I'm sore, hungry and thirstier than I've ever been before, too parched even to cry.

And cold as well. A nasty spring rain falls hard upon us as we travel. The wind blows the rain through the bars, soaking me to the bone. "My laird, might I please have some water, and perhaps a cloak? 'Tis awfully bitter back here," I croak to the soldier through the thick metal grate at the front of the wagon.

"Maybe when we stop, for the night," he answers sharply, "but only if you keep your gob shut and behave yourself 'til then."

Obediently, I stay silent until the skies darken, and the wagon finally creaks to a halt beside a small copse of trees, a stream babbling merrily beside it. When the door swings open, I nearly faint with relief. It has been raining for most of the day, but now the rain has finally ceased, and I can see several stars twinkle between the clouds in the evening sky overhead.

"This is as far as we go tonight. You've got two minutes to go about your business then get back inside the wagon for the night. Behave and you'll get a drink and a bite to eat. If not, you'll get nothing for your troubles but a sound thrashing, do you understand?"

"Aye, my laird," I reply hoarsely, my throat aching with thirst. "Do ye think ye could possibly take these locks off my hands and feet? It's so hard to move and they hurt terribly. I won't run away, I swear it. I cannae hardly walk as it is."

"I ain't s'posed to," he replies uncertainly, looking at me closely for the first time. "Orders. Still, you're just a little girl, ain't you? Not much older than me own granddaughter at home." The soldier weighs his options carefully as I wait in silence.

"All right, then," he finally says, taking the keys out of his belt, "I'll free your feet, but I don't dare unlock your hands with you out of the wagon. The colonel would have me flayed if I did."

He inserts the keys and the shackles fall off my ankles. "There you go," he says as he points meaningfully to his pistol tucked into his belt, "but stay close or . . ."

I fully understand the threat. On aching legs, I step behind a small bush to do my *business* as he calls it, then I walk slowly to the stream and plunge my hands into the delicious water. The water seeps under the iron manacles and cools my skin as I wash the grime from my face and then drink deeply from the stream until my belly can hold no more water.

Wild thoughts run through my mind. The soldier is an old man and even with my hands chained I could outrun him. The creek runs through a farmer's field, and beyond that?

Who knows what I would find? A small village, perhaps, and a friendly blacksmith who would shelter me for the night and take off my chains?

I start to edge toward the field then stop. Perhaps I may find freedom and help but it is just as likely I'll encounter another person eager to betray me for a few coins. Besides, the soldier showed me a small act of mercy when he released my legs, and I did give him my word I wouldn't run. I've never been the sort of person to break a promise or betray a kindness, no matter what.

Reluctantly, I return to the wagon. "Thank ye, my laird," I say. I still shiver from the cold but feel much better for the drink.

"Nicholas," my guard replies, with a softness in his voice I haven't heard before.

"Excuse me, my laird?"

"Name's Nicholas, missy, Nicholas Potts. You don't have to call me sir, laird, or none of that fancy stuff. I'm just a simple old soldier."

Potts gives me a thick woollen blanket. Once I wrap it around my shoulders he passes me a small wicker basket as well. "You'll warm up soon enough, and if you're hungry I have bread and cold ham. It's me own supper, but you look like you need it more than I do. Besides, I wouldn't feed the rubbish they gave me for you to a pig."

The chain jangles as I grab the food and eat hungrily, hardly bothering to chew. "Slow down," laughs Potts. "You're liable to choke eatin' like that!"

"And what if I do?" I say bitterly. "They're going to hang me when we get to London, aren't they? That's what the colonel said."

Potts is sympathetic. "I don't know for certain, missy, but it don't look good for you, that's for sure. Newgate's not a place I'd ever want to go."

"What is this Newgate?" I ask. "I dinnae ken it. The English colonel said that was my destination, but I've never heard of the place in my life."

"Oh missy," says Potts. "You might be better off not knowing. Newgate's a gaol in London. *The* gaol you might say, where the really bad 'uns go to meet their end."

"But why send me there?" On the verge of tears, the reality of my situation rapidly catches up to me. "I've done naught wrong!"

"To be honest I agree with you. I heard what your brother did, and I can see why he'd be hanged if he were pinched, but you? I know the colonel said you would be the one to suffer for your brother's crimes since he escaped, but it seems a rather harsh price to pay, guilty of nothing more than being his sister and going for a run on the docks. How old are you, by the way?"

The question seems strange to me. "I'm fourteen and a half. Why?"

"You look younger than that," Potts says, "so when you get to Newgate and they put you on trial, tell the judge you're twelve. Then blame your brother for everything that happened and beg 'em for mercy. That's what I'd do."

"I willna do that! It's not the truth at all." I cry at the repugnant suggestion.

"My dear," Potts says gently, "English justice has little room for the truth. What you say won't make no difference to your brother, but with a bit of luck it will be enough to save your life. After all, they don't execute children at Newgate near as much as they used to."

Chapter 10

THE ROAD TO LONDON is bumpy and rutted, and the wagon bounces roughly over every pothole, jarring my body until I feel as if my very bones will shatter. Potts feels sorry for me, has even grown fond of me, I think. He keeps the manacles off my feet and wrists as we travel slowly south, has given me a blanket at night, and as much fresh food as he can, but no kind deed the soldier does can change the fact that the three-day trip to London, locked in the back of the prison wagon, is one of the most terrible experiences of my life.

The horses' feet and the wheels of the wagon kick up mud and water that splashes into the wagon, and between that and the mist and rain, I'm always cold, wet and chilled to the bone. "This is our last night on the road, Missy," Potts announces that night. "We shall reach London tomorrow."

"And then what? Locked away in an awful gaol until I'm taken to trial and hanged?" As terrible as the road has been, at least I've been able to breathe fresh air and see the sky overhead.

"Not if I can help it," says Potts suddenly. "Miss Libby, hold up your hands."

"Mr. Potts, Nicholas?" I'm not sure what the soldier is trying to say.

"I can't stand the thought of your getting locked up in Newgate. I don't want no part of it and I won't have your blood on my hands, as they say."

Potts takes the keyring that dangles on his belt and slips a large key into my manacles. "I'll say you overpowered me, that you escaped," he says excitedly. Then he holds out his gun. "Take my pistol and knock me on the head with it. It will make the story more believable. You'll be a fugitive again, but at least you'll have a chance."

The chains fall off my wrists, but I don't move. "And what will happen to me should the army find me again?"

Potts hesitates. "Hanged as an escaped prisoner for certain," he says reluctantly. "But only if you're caught. The army will send troops out looking for you, but they won't expect you to go to London. I'd make for Shepherd's Bush or Camden if I were you. There's a great many Irish and Scots who live there. The army would never find you."

"And what will happen to ye, should I run as ye'd have me do?"

"A good talking to, perhaps a day or two behind bars. A flogging at worst," he says. "All worth it to see an innocent girl saved."

I don't believe a word of it. "There is no chance Colonel Phillips would believe I escaped. I'm supposed to be locked inside a wagon with chains on my hands and feet. He'll know ye took them off and what would happen to ye then?"

Potts answers even more reluctantly than when he talked about my possible fate. "If Colonel Phillips truly believed I helped you? A general court martial most likely on any number of charges."

"Then ye'd be hanged yerself. Don't ye lie to me, Nicholas Potts. Tell me the truth."

"Not hanged," the soldier says reluctantly. "Hanging's reserved for civilians. I'd be shot."

I've heard enough. I pick up the manacles and with a solid click lock them back up onto my wrists. "I'll not see anyone hurt because of me. Ye cannae do this, I willna let ye. I'll take my chances with British justice, such as it is. After all, they dinnae hang children nearly as much as they used to, right?"

Chapter 11

THE WEATHER HAS CHANGED for the better, and though the night is warm I hardly rest at all. My scattered bits of sleep are full of terrible nightmares of the scaffold, the rope, and the evil grin of the hangman. I dream of the noose slipping over my head, and the last thing I see before I drop off to sleep is the face of my brother watching helpless, anguished in the middle of the cheering crowd.

I awake from my nightmare just before dawn breaks. We move on, and just as with Glasgow, I smell London long before we reach the heart of the city. Through the bars I watch the country lanes widen into large streets, streets in turn that lead us to the middle of a metropolis that dwarfs the grimy

Scottish city I used to call home after we were forced from Loch Tay.

"Almost there," Potts says as the wagon grinds to a halt on a busy street. "Last chance, missy. Say the word and I'll set you free."

"Ye'll do no such thing," I tell him. "I'll not have yer blood on my hands."

"In that case, remember what I said when we get to Newgate; you're a young impressionable girl who did as she was told by her brute of a brother."

Potts steps back to the front of the wagon and takes the reins in his hands. "Just a little bit further now. Less than a mile down Newgate Street to the prison gates, then we're there.

"And one last thing," he says as the prison wagon creaks to a stop. "No matter what happens, you must be brave. You may be terrified, but don't show it to the animals inside those walls. If they think you're weak, then you're a gonner for sure."

For a moment there is silence, but then I hear harsh voices from outside the wagon, and I fight to control the panic rising in my throat when footsteps, much heavier ones than Nicholas Potts ever produced, thump loudly towards me. "Be brave, Libby," Potts says softly. "You must be brave."

A key jingles, then slides noisily into the lock. I tremble as the door is thrown open by a hulking man who drags me out of the wagon, depositing me hard onto the ground.

"I would have gotten out myself if ye'd asked," I say, trying to be courageous as Potts said. I stand up and face the man, an act more difficult than I'd realized with my feet still in irons.

The man slaps me hard against the face, with enough force that I rock back on my heels, almost falling. "Prisoners don' speak 'til spoken to," he says in a strange accent. "You're a bold one, ain't ya? Well, I wonder 'ow brave and strong you'll be after a week or so in 'ere! Me name is 'Obbes. There's many rules at Newgate. My job is to 'elp you learn 'em all."

The man called Hobbes leans in closely. My head aches, and I feel sick from both the blow and the stench of him. Hobbes is a tall, lumbering brute with thin stringy yellow hair, a large crooked nose, massive arms and an ample belly. A short, wooden club dangles from his belt. His teeth are black and rotten, his breath full of the smell of beer and onions. "Oh yes, me pretty. We'll find out what sort o' stuff you're made of, soon enough, won't we?"

I take in my surroundings. Newgate Prison is almost as frightening a sight as Hobbes: a massive bulk of thick grey-red stone, heavy wooden doors and iron bars. Even the bright spring sun seems no match to the dark shadows the prison casts on the street.

Hobbes unlocks my feet then grabs my hands, pulling me towards a thick oak door. "Help me, Nicholas!" I cry, suddenly regretting that I'd not taken the kind soldier up on his offer to release me, but there is nothing he can do except look sadly as Hobbes opens the door and pushes me inside.

We enter a dark, narrow hallway. Hobbes walks quickly, and I struggle to keep up, tripping several times as we traverse a maze of gloomy passages, travelling deeper and deeper into the bowels of the prison. "Oi! Turnkey! Let me keep 'er company a little while!" yells a voice from the darkness of a cell.

"No! She's mine!" croaks a leering face from another. "It's me birthday! I want to 'ave 'er as a present!" Dirty hands reach out between the iron bars, clutching at my arm as we pass by.

"Back to your 'oles, vermin!" bellows Hobbes. He swings his club, and I hear a sickening wet *crrack* as it connects on the prisoner's outstretched arm. "I like teachin' lessons," Hobbes says, as the prisoner shrieks in pain and lets go of my sleeve. "I taught 'im not to do that again, didn't I?"

A few moments later we reach a cell door and stop. Hobbes takes the key ring from his belt, unlocks the iron door and shoves me into a small, dark chamber. "What's going to happen to me now?" I instantly regret opening my mouth as Hobbes' ham-sized palm smacks into the side of my head once more.

"I said prisoners don' speak till spoken to. You don' remember your lessons too well neither, it seems, but since you asked so nice, I don' mind tellin' you that this is one of the condemned cells. Enjoy it, missy, 'cause this comfy little corner of Newgate will be your 'ome till your trial at the Old Bailey. And who knows when that'll be? Court's a little backed up at the moment, you see."

The gaoler leaves the cell, slamming the door behind him, turning the key in the lock with a loud click. "Your turn will come soon enough. Maybe next week. Maybe next year. Till then I'll be mindin' you while you bide your time 'ere."

I stand frozen in place until a soft voice from somewhere in the darkness behind startles me. "This is your first day in Newgate by the looks of you, I'd wager," it says. "Me? I've been 'ere two 'undred and seventy-eight. Welcome to New-gate Prison, my dear. Welcome to 'ell."

I choke back a cry as a faint shape emerges from the black shadows of the cell. It's a woman, a girl really, not much older than myself, I see with relief when she enters the weak light that comes through the bars on the door. Her hair is long and dirty. She wears a dark cotton dress, ripped and even filthier than her hair. "Me name's Clara Willoughby, from Stepney. Who are you?"

"Elizabeth Scott, but people call me Libby," I reply, regaining my composure.

"Well then, my little Scottish lassie," Clara asks. "What terrible crime did you commit to end up in the clink?"

"I . . . I dinnae ken." Despite my best efforts to be strong, the terror of the day has finally caught up to me.

"There, there, you'll be all right." I collapse to the ground, weeping uncontrollably. Clara kneels beside me, puts my head on her lap and gently strokes my hair.

"Cry, Libby Scott," Clara says. "Cry 'til all the tears 'ave left your eyes, then don't you never weep in this place again.

Today is the first of many sad days in Newgate. You'll need to find a way to be brave because, believe you me, this is just the beginnin' of your misery."

Chapter 12

"SO, TELL ME YOUR STORY, Libby," says Clara, when my tears subside. "You don't much look like a felon to me."

"My parents are dead," I say, wiping my eyes, "and that was when it started." Clara and I sit in the darkness and talk. We are on our beds, such as they are. There are no mattresses or pillows in our cell, just piles of rags and old blankets that have been here for years, judging by the look — and the smell of them.

I haven't talked about my family to anyone since the day I said goodbye to Duncan in Liverpool, but today I tell Clara all about our eviction, our terrible life in Glasgow, the fire, the trek to England, and our betrayal by Tinker. The events seem distant, like wisps of a half-remembered dream.

"And where's your brother now?" Clara asks. "What happened to 'im after the soldiers took you?"

"On a ship called *The Leopard*, bound for Boston." With a price on Duncan's head, I'll not give up the truth to anyone. "He's gone."

"I lost someone I loved, too," Clara says. Then, despite her own admonition about not crying, large tears roll down her cheeks. "Me son. 'Is name was Peter."

I'm shocked. "Clara! Ye have a wee bairn? Ye cannae be much older than I!"

Clara smiles. "I was sixteen when Peter was born. He weren't exactly planned, as they say, but I loved 'im very much. He was a beautiful little boy, with a thick shock of black 'air and a smile that would melt your 'eart. He was always happy — right until 'e got sick, that was."

Clara pauses to catch her composure. "It started as a cough, then Peter caught a fever and it wouldna break. I tried to get 'im 'elp but I didn't 'ave no money, so the doctor refused to see 'im. There 'e was, my baby, gettin' thinner and thinner, the life slowly leavin' 'is eyes, the poor soul. I was desperate."

My heart breaks for my new friend. "What did ye do?"

"Nothin' more than any mother would do. I needed money, so I broke into the 'ouse of a shopkeeper to find some, but he was 'ome and I got pinched. The judge found me guilty of robbery in all of five minutes, then sent me 'ere."

"And Peter? What happened to him?"

Clara takes a moment to wipe her tears before continuing. "Died in 'is grandmother's arms the day after my arrest. At least that's what they told me. Poor little boy never even 'ad a chance to see 'is second birthday. I wasn't there when he passed, but that's all right, because I'll see 'im soon enough in Heaven. I'm to be 'anged by the neck 'til dead. It's taken 'em long enough to carry out the sentence, but carry it out they will."

"That's awful!" I cry. "When?"

"Tomorrow," Clara says flatly. "I will die tomorrow."

Chapter 13

"IT'S TIME, MISSY!" bellows Hobbes, thudding the butt of his club onto the thick iron door of our cell. "You've got an appointment with the 'angman and 'e 'ates to be kept waitin'!" Hobbes seems happy, almost gleeful at Clara's impending death, but I feel ill at the sound of the jailor's voice.

"Can I 'ave just one more minute?" Clara pleads.

"I suppose so," Hobbes replies munificently. "Consider it your last request."

"Listen carefully, Libby," whispers Clara. "There's a wealthy Quaker lady who comes to Newgate from time to time. Her name's Elizabeth Fry. She's taken us prisoners up as 'er cause, 'specially the women and the children in 'ere who ain't did nothin' much wrong. She tried to 'elp me but 'er pleas fell on deaf ears. There ain't much sympathy in London for a thief like me, even one who only tried to save 'er baby's life."

"Clara, dinnae talk like that," I protest, but she quickly cuts me off.

"This ain't no time for arguin'. I'm gonna swing, but you're innocent, you are. Elizabeth Fry will find out about you. She'll 'elp, I just know she will. It's too late for me, but you still 'ave a chance."

"Minute's up!" says Hobbes impatiently. "Time to meet your maker."

Clara hugs me tightly. "Don't worry 'bout me, Libby. I ain't sad to say goodbye to this life; the next one can only be better."

Clara lets go of me, then holds out her hands for Hobbes' waiting handcuffs. "Let's get this over with, 'Obbes. There's a little boy waitin' for 'is ma."

"The only person waitin' for you is Brunskill the 'angman," chortles the gaoler.

"And don't you shed no tears, you little Scottish wretch," he tells me. "Your time's comin' soon enough. Sir Simon Le Blanc's trying your case from what I 'ear. Of all the judges on the King's Bench, no one sends more to the gallows than 'im. I've a feelin' you'll be seein' your little friend again — and much sooner than you'd like."

Chapter 14

❧

"DID YOU MISS ME?" Hobbes snickers as the cell door creaks open. I've endured many long and lonely nights without a visit from anyone since Clara was taken, and though I long for company, I want nothing to do with this awful man.

I glare as Hobbes approaches, but stay silent, wise enough not to respond as the gaoler clamps a set of manacles around my wrists and pulls me into the hallway. "Still a brave little thing, I see," he cackles. "Well, let's see 'ow far that goes with Sir Simon. Your trial's tomorrow, but I've been ordered to take you to the court 'ouse now."

Hobbes marches me down the hallway until we reach a small, wooden door. "Us turnkeys call this passage the

Graveyard," he says, opening the door to reveal a dark tunnel beyond. He strolls into the blackness as casually as if we were walking down a country lane.

"It's a safe little passage from Newgate to the Ol' Bailey. It's got another use, too. Executed prisoners are taken down from the gallows then buried down 'ere beneath the floor. Usually nobody wants their bodies when they die, see, so we do 'em that last kindness."

Hobbes points to two letters carved roughly into a flagstone above a freshly dug grave as we walk. "Ave a look. It's a little dark to see 'em proper from this distance, but those are grave markers, they are. Everyone gets a Christian burial at Newgate — even your wicked cellmate."

I bend down and choke back a cry when I see the "C.W." freshly etched into the grey surface of the flagstone, freshly disturbed dirt beside it.

"Clara?"

"Yes! Clara! You're a smart one, ain't ya, knowin' your letters and all! What a surprise it must be for you, runnin' into your little friend like this! She said someone was waitin' for 'er before she dangled. I wonder if she found 'em under that stone?"

"Yer an evil man!" I cry, about to say much more until Hobbes' hand shoots out like a viper. He grabs me by the neck, pulling my face towards his until we are only inches apart.

"You don' know what evil is," he hisses, his rancid breath

making me gag. "I'd teach you that lesson 'ere and now if I had my way, but lucky for you the judge don' like 'is prisoners damaged before 'e gets to see 'em."

"How lucky fer me." I'm too angry to be scared. Instead of the expected hit, however, Hobbes lets me go, his rotten mouth breaking into a wide grin.

"Lucky? No missy, you ain't lucky at all. Sir Simon may want his prisoners untouched before their trials, but afterwards? Now that's a different story. Know this, missy. I promise that before you swing, you'll learn that there are far worse things in Newgate than death."

Chapter 15

❧

HOBBES UNLOCKS ANOTHER heavy iron door at the far end of the Graveyard. I squint as we step out of the tunnel and onto a cobblestoned street. It has been weeks since I've seen the sky, and the sunlight feels like flames burning in my eyes.

"The Ol' Bailey's just a few steps down the street," he says, as my eyes adjust to the light. The *street* Hobbes refers to is little more than a narrow alley, lined with a tall brick wall on either side. We are the only two people I can see.

A grand boulevard ain't it?" snickers Hobbes. "Made this way on purpose; the walls allow for a nice and peaceful stroll without bein' seen by the public. It's all quiet now, but in a few 'ours the streets on the other side of the wall will be full.

The daily executions start first thing in the mornin', and people do like to come out for the show. I wager there will be a fine crowd when you drop. You're quite the celebrity, you are."

We reach the Old Bailey. The courthouse is a foreboding, squat brick building with two uniformed guards standing in front of a large wooden door. "She's all yours, lads," says Hobbes, as the court gaolers take me by my arms.

The wooden door creaks open. Hobbes tilts his neck at a strange angle then sticks out his tongue. Don't worry. I'll see you again soon, missy, though you won't be seein' me."

"But do us a favour, won't you?" he asks before the door closes behind me. "If you do happen to meet your little friend after your neck snaps, tell 'er 'Obbes sends 'is love."

The door shuts behind Hobbes as the gaolers lead me down a steep flight of stairs. At the bottom I see a series of small cells, three with people locked inside them.

"This lot are waiting to have their day in court," says one of the guards, a thin, sallow man with heavy sideburns and walrus moustache. "We're laying down bets on their sentences, ain't we, Paul?"

"We certainly are, Andrew, me mate," says the other, a lumpy, pear-shaped man with a bald head. He jerks his finger towards a cell where an old, confused-looking man appears to be talking to himself.

"That mad one? He pinched a pair of shoes off a cart in Whitechapel. He'll earn a date with the gallows for his crimes.

Bedlam is stuffed full at the moment, so dangling is the next best option. Don't want the crazies wandering the streets, do we?"

"And that vicious-looking creature over there?" Andrew jabs his finger to a weeping young woman in the cell next to the shoe thief. "She's a scullery maid, guilty of the felonious takin' of her mistress's hat. Paul thinks she'll be transported to Botany Bay for fifteen years, but I wager she'll swing."

"You think she's going to die because she stole a hat?" I ask. It seems such a terribly harsh punishment for such a small crime.

"It was a very nice hat," chortles Andrew. "Feathers, ribbons, everything. Her mistress was quite fond of it. Very cross she was to have it taken. Her husband is a Member of Parliament. Guaranteed, Sir Simon sentences her to death."

"And don't you let that one's pretty looks fool you," says Andrew as we pass the third prisoner, a handsome young man in his late twenties, who smiles and gives me a slight bow from behind the bars as we approach.

"He's the worst of the lot by far and there's no doubt the hangman is waiting for him. Was a coachman in some rich banker's house. A trusted, loyal servant, member of the family until he took their only daughter for a ride in the coach to enjoy a nice spring day. Lovely little thing she was. Younger than you I'd wager, missy, but just as pretty."

"They found her floating in the Thames a week later," says Andrew. "After the wretch stole her purse, he slit the little miss's throat and threw her in the river. We're expecting a large crowd in the Old Bailey today."

The guard named Paul unlocks the iron door of a cell and shoves me in. "But that spectacle ain't nothing compared to what's gonna happen when you enter the court tomorrow morning."

"Why me?" I have no idea what the gaoler with the pale face is talking about.

"Good gracious, missy!" he exclaims, taking the iron manacles off my wrists. "You don't mean to tell us you don't know? You're famous, you are, and that fugitive brother of yours, too."

Paul talks as if he can't believe his good fortune. "This is all very exciting for us turnkeys, having you here. Attacking a man like Sir Cecil Hamilton? He's like the king's fifth cousin or something. All the newspapers will be sending their men to cover your trial. It will be the event of the year at the Old Bailey and we'll have front-row tickets!"

Chapter 16

I AM LOCKED INTO a small cell with no window. When the guards walk away with their lanterns I am left in the dark alone, save for the whistling of the murderer, the gentle weeping of the scullery maid and the mad chatter of the shoe thief. Those sounds end some hours later when the gaolers return, unlock their cages and walk the prisoners out of the cells. After that, I am utterly alone, left to contemplate my awful fate in the darkness of the cell.

"Rise and shine, dearie!" Despite my situation with both my hands and feet still locked in irons, I must have fallen asleep. I slowly come back to my senses as lantern light floods my cell. "Sir Simon's waiting for you," the guard called Paul says as he unlocks the door. Confused and terrified, I stumble up a set of stairs, down a stone hallway to a small wooden door.

"Show time," Andrew chortles, opening the door. "Do us proud, won't you?"

When I enter the packed court, the chatter of conversation ends immediately, replaced by whispers and hushed murmurs. Guided by the guards, I walk unsteadily to the prisoner's dock, chains jangling, acutely aware that I am the centre of attention.

I take my place in the prisoner's dock then stare at the handful of black-robed clerks and lawyers who huddle around a large, felt-covered table in the centre of the courtroom, talking to each other and writing notes.

When the courthouse is silent, a bailiff begins the proceedings in a crisp, officious manner. "All rise! The court is now in session. The honourable Justice Simon Le Blanc presiding."

Sir Simon is a severe-looking old man in elegant, red fur robes and a white powdered wig. He casts a glare so terrifying as he walks in and takes his seat in front of me that I wish the ground would open and swallow me up whole.

"Elizabeth Scott," the bailiff says once Sir Simon is ready. "It is alleged by the Crown that not only did you assist your brother Duncan Scott in his vicious and unprovoked attempted murder of Sir Cecil Hamilton, but that you also aided him in his flight from the King's armed forces in

Liverpool, and then fled from justice yourself. These are
capital offences. How do you plead?"

I don't respond. I can't. I'm too dazed, still trying to orient
myself to these strange surroundings. "Answer the question,
girl: how do you plead?" says Sir Simon Le Blanc.

"My laird, I've done naught wrong." I manage to find my
words, the same words that resulted in a fierce blow from
Colonel Phillips back in Liverpool.

"The prisoner pleads not guilty," announces the bailiff as
the audience claps approvingly. A not guilty plea means a
trial, and my guards have told me that Sir Simon's cases are
very entertaining — for the spectators at least.

To my right is the jury. Some of the twelve men listen
intently, while others talk to each other, seemingly ignoring
the proceedings. It gives me little hope that one of the men
gathered to judge my fate, a fat man with his powdered wig
resting sideways on his head, leans back in his chair, snoring
loudly.

The trial is a farce from the beginning. I listen in shocked
disbelief as the crown's barrister begins the proceedings by
reading Sir Cecil Hamilton's testimony.

The mill owner is not at the Old Bailey, of course. I was
told to expect that by the guards. Men of Hamilton's stature
rarely attend these trials as their written statements are con-
sidered more than enough.

"'As soon as I heard of the fire I rode to the factory,'" reads
the clerk. "'I was worried about my business, of course, but

the fate of the people working for me was first and foremost in my mind. When I arrived to see the place fully ablaze, I did what I could.

"'I was helping an old fellow who'd come out of the burning building, when suddenly I felt a blinding pain in my head. A young Scottish lass, Elizabeth Scott, I learned later, hit me from behind, then pushed me to the ground.'"

The crowd howls. What sort of villain must they think I am to do such a thing to a knight of the realm, especially one who was valiantly helping his workers?

When the audience recovers its composure, the clerk continues reading Hamilton's fabricated testimony: "It was at that time her brother, a murderous creature, attacked me as well, and with my own walking stick too. Time and time again he beat me as the girl urged him on. 'Kill him,' she said, 'bash his brains out!' Mercifully I was knocked unconscious and then the beatings stopped. I supposed he thought he'd finished me."

More shouts erupt from the jury. The sleeping fat man is now fully awake, his ruddy cheeks jiggling with outrage. Shame!" he cries, slamming his meaty fists indignantly into the wooden railing. "Shame!"

"Nae! It's not true!" I plead. "None of it!"

Sir Simon bangs his gavel loudly on the desk. "The prisoner will be silent! I will have order in this courtroom!"

When the crowd reluctantly settles down, the clerk reads a statement from Colonel Phillips, the officer in Liverpool who'd sent me to Newgate, all the while reporters from numerous newspapers hurriedly scribble down their notes.

In terse, military language, Phillips' statement recounts how I'd sent Duncan off on the *Leopard* to evade capture, ran away myself and was caught only because the crippled sailor Will betrayed me before I could board the *Elsa* for Dublin.

Although Colonel Phillips didn't know that the first part of his testimony about the *Leopard* is wrong, there is no denying the fact I ran and was turned over to the soldiers before I could leave England myself. The only person in the courtroom who knows that Duncan did not escape on the *Leopard* is me, and I must stay silent on that part for my brother's sake.

The jurors shake their head as they listen, speaking to each other in angry tones. "And so, my lord," the crown's barrister concludes, "we have incontrovertible proof that this impudent woman allowed her brother to escape justice. At least," he grins, "she *thought* he escaped justice."

The lawyer picks up a piece of paper and waves it over his head dramatically. The chatter stops immediately. This is an unexpected development; spectators and court officials alike strain to hear.

He pauses for effect then smiles at the crowded courtroom. "The arm of the British Empire is long — but our Lord's reach is further still. I hold in my hand a dispatch from the Admiralty." The audience is silent. I wonder just what on earth this has to do with my trial.

"An American merchant ship came upon wreckage in the North Atlantic, near Newfoundland," he reads. "They found an empty life boat, as well as other flotsam floating on the sea, later identified as coming from the migrant ship *Leopard*. They passed the information to the captain of a Royal Navy Frigate en route to Halifax, who patrolled the area further and found several bodies and additional debris floating on the surface of the Atlantic."

The crown's lawyer, pauses and looks around the courtroom, like an actor holding the crowd in the palm of his hand. "Yes," he continues, "Duncan Scott may have fled English justice, but he did not escape the wrath of the Almighty; he lies dead at the bottom of the Atlantic Ocean, his body entombed in a watery grave within the wreckage of the *Leopard*."

The court cheers madly. This is a spectacular development indeed, judging by their reaction. "Order! Order in my court!" commands Le Blanc. While I pity those who'd perished, I also feel a slight twinge of hope. I know now that my brother is completely safe, wherever he is. If the Redcoats thinks Duncan is dead, they'll not bother looking for him. My sacrifice has been worth it, no matter what happens to me now.

The lawyer jabs an accusatory finger towards me. "And as if you needed more proof of this girl's black heart, just look at her! She's just been told her brother's dead, drowned alongside a score of innocent souls, but where is her emotion? Where is her sadness? Not one tear does she shed! Instead, she sits there with a repugnant smile on her face!"

Sir Simon faces the jury and addresses them over the jeers and boos that rise anew from the audience. "Gentlemen. You may now retire to consider your verdict."

With dismay I realize the trial is over. I haven't been asked to testify, haven't told my story, haven't even been afforded the opportunity to tell the lie Potts suggested to save my life. The jurors step outside and confer briefly. Then they return.

"We have reached a verdict, my lord," says their spokesman as the crowd roars again. The trial certainly has lived up to their expectations.

When the commotion subsides, Le Blanc's voice rings out across the courtroom. "What is your decision?"

"Guilty, my lord, guilty."

The jury's decision rendered, Le Blanc peers down at me. I feel as if the very wind has been sucked out of my lungs as a terrible smile creases his face.

I watch in confusion as he places a piece of what looks to be black silk on top of his head. I don't know what it's for but judging by the applause that rolls around the courtroom, the spectators and officials most certainly do.

Simon Le Blanc's wooden gavel thunders down on the wooden desk. "Elizabeth Scott," he says, as silence descends onto the courtroom. "It is now my terrible duty to pass judgment upon you." I can hardly hear him speak through the thunderstorm rolling in my head.

"You will be taken hence to the prison in which you were last confined. From there you will go to the place of execution where you will be hanged by the neck until you are dead, and thereafter your body buried within the precincts of the prison. May the Lord have mercy upon your soul."

Chapter 17

ON THE SUNDAY MORNING before my execution, the New-gate prison chapel is full. The chapel is a large stone chamber, lit with pale morning light that streams in through the barred windows. At the front is the pulpit: a raised wooden dais accessible by a wooden staircase.

In the middle of the chapel is the condemned pew, a black pen-like structure, big enough to hold two dozen people or more. Today there are only twelve, including me: two older women, eight men and a ginger-haired boy younger than me. Beside each of us is a coffin — the same coffins we'll be buried in after our executions tomorrow.

I sit next to an older woman named Mary Barrington.

This is not, I've learned, the first time Mary has been in this chapel. "Spent half of me fifty years in Newgate for one thing or another," Mary tells me as we wait for the sermon to begin.

"But I'll be leavin' for good tomorrow, same as you. This time they got me for impersonatin' a lady and buyin' things under her name at the dressmakers. Guess the judge got sick of seein' me face so he made sure I wouldna be comin' back to his courtroom no more."

I only half-listen. Instead, my attention is riveted to the rectangular box beside me. My coffin is made of rough-cut wood. I will be lying dead within it this time tomorrow. It is the most awful thing I've ever seen.

"See them over there?" says Mary, indicating a crowd of one hundred or so manacled men and women, dressed in rags, standing behind and to the sides of the condemned pew. "They're Newgate prisoners, come to listen to the sermon. We're to serve as examples, to make 'em change their ways before they end up like us."

Mary laughs bitterly. "Didn' work so good for me, though. I've 'eard three condemned sermons before today, standin' right where they are. P'raps I should have paid better attention."

"Those up there dinnae seem like prisoners," I say, looking at a crowd of well-dressed spectators sitting in what looks to be a balcony.

"They ain't. The fat one on the left is the Sheriff. He's the one who organizes the executions. The tall one with the beaky nose is John Kirby, the Chief Keeper of Newgate Prison 'imself, while the uniformed ones are court officials. The rest are well-to-does. They pay good money to come and listen to the sermon — and to get a close-up look at us. They'll be outside the Debtor's Door tomorrow as well, sittin' on cushions and eatin' sweetmeats while we dangle. Nothin' but entertainment for them. We are no different than dogfights or 'orse racin'."

"Who's that?" I ask. Beside John Kirby is a tall, distinguished-looking man in a black suit, a tall black top hat on his head.

"That one? No idea. Some lord or somethin', in the government, no doubt wanting to come and see justice served."

The murmurs cease as a middle-aged, heavyset robed priest enters the chapel and climbs slowly up the wooden staircase to the pulpit. "Let us sing," the man begins, as the crowd, condemned prisoners and spectators alike, get to their feet.

"That one's Reverend Cotton," explains Mary. "The Ordinary of Newgate. It's his job to prepare our souls for Heaven — if that's where we're goin'."

When the hymn ends, Cotton turns to the condemned pew. "Louis Languis and Joseph Westwood. Guilty of forgery." Cotton's voice is deep and languorous as it echoes off the stone walls of the chapel.

"Herbert Watkins. Guilty of highway robbery. John Holloway and Owen Haggarty. Guilty of murder," he says, looking at each of the prisoners in turn. "Patrick Danville. Guilty of theft." The boy sobs and my heart breaks for him. His crime? Stealing coal for the brazier to warm his small home where he lived with his widowed mother.

Some of the prisoners hang their heads as their crimes are reported. Others, like Owen Haggarty, stare defiantly, even smiling at Cotton as he reads his name.

"Mary Barrington, impersonation."

"I'm innocent, me lord!" she says with an air of seriousness. "It weren't me; it was somebody impersonatin' me! Besides, I plead the belly!"

Cotton scowls at Mary as the crowd erupts in laughter. "Mary Barrington, you have been found guilty as charged, and you are most certainly not with child. You would be better served confessing and repenting than wasting what little time you have left on this earth with lies."

"Worth a try," grins Mary.

"Elizabeth Scott." Cotton's gaze is now fixed firmly on me. "Attempted murder, aiding a felon, evading the King's justice." Cotton stands up straight, sweeping his hand towards us.

"Repent and confess; there is still time to save your eternal souls." Cotton then opens a prayer book. "We will now commence with the Burial Service."

"We're lucky in a way," says Mary. "Usually people die before their burial service, but we get to 'ear it while there's still breath in our lungs. There ain't much time for ceremony outside on the gallows tomorrow, you see, so they like to do it 'ere."

"I am the resurrection and the life, saith the Lord," intones Cotton, the crowd following along to the well-known words. "He that believeth in me, though he were dead, yet shall he live: and whosoever liveth and believeth in me, shall never die."

My mind wanders as my eyes drift back to my coffin. I scarcely hear the Ordinary read the prayer, lead the congregation in another hymn, then settle into the condemned sermon, a terrible rant full of fire and brimstone and everlasting suffering. No words can be worse than seeing the box you will be buried in, picturing your own flesh rotting, your bones turning slowly to dust.

Mercifully, the service soon ends. "That was awful," I say as we are led out of the chapel in irons, back to our cells. "I never want to listen to that man again."

"Then I 'ave some bad news for you," says Mary. "Reverend Cotton will be presidin' over our executions tomorrow and the last sound you'll 'ear before you drop is 'is voice, sendin' you off into the afterlife."

Chapter 18

∽

"GONNA BE QUITE THE spectacle today," Hobbes announces, swinging open the door of my cell. "Crowd's been growing since dawn. Your 'angin' might well be the best draw of the year!"

My hanging. Today is Monday the seventh of July 1807. The last day of my life. My legs buckle at the thought of it. I fall to my knees onto the cold floor, my guts heaving. I've had precious little to eat since my trial, but what food there is makes its way back up my throat and splashes down onto the stones.

Hobbes pulls me to my feet and puts my hands and feet in irons. As he does, he laughs, an evil cackle that bounces off the walls. "Ain't so brave now, are you, missy? I said you'd learn some lessons in 'ere; time to learn your last one. Don't worry though," he says, removing me from the cell for the last time. You'll 'ave your brother and that mate of yours waitin' for you. Old Nick too, I'd wager. Gonna be nice and hot where you're goin'. Scum like you don't see no pearly gates!"

Hobbes takes me outside into the press yard, a narrow stone enclosure surrounded by high walls with sharp metal spikes built into the stones on the top of the wall, a last defence should, by some miracle, a condemned prisoner makes it that high in a futile attempt at escape.

Summer is here, but there is no sun. The sky above is dark, thick with rain-swollen clouds. Large drops fall onto the square flagstones of the yard. Puddles have already formed in the depressions, with the promise of more to come.

The other condemned prisoners are present in the yard as well. Louis Languis and Joseph Westwood, the forgers, sit together on a bench, talking quietly. Herbert Watkins, the highwayman stands alone. Patrick Danville and John Holloway, the murderers, weep loudly, ignored by the turnkeys who have Owen Haggarty, trussed up tightly with ropes as well as his irons.

Still defiant, Haggarty must have put up a struggle by the looks of things. His right eye is swollen shut, blood runs freely down his forehead, a wound no doubt caused by the guard's wooden truncheon.

"Mornin', Libby," says Mary Barrington. Mary seems much

more subdued than yesterday. She isn't cracking jokes or smiling, not anymore. "Not a nice day for an execution, but then again what is? Maybe the weather will keep the looky-loos away, and we can 'ave a respectful end."

"No chance of that, you old crone," mutters Hobbes. "Like I said before, today's a 'igh point on the calendar for the mob. Listen, out there, on the other side of the Debtor's Door. Can you 'ear 'em?" The Debtor's Door is a large entryway of solid iron, built into the stone bulk of the prison. Despite myself I strain to listen. Sure enough, from the other side of the wall I hear the chatter of the crowd.

"Remove their irons," commands a familiar voice.

"Told you you'd 'ear 'im again," whispers Mary as Reverend Cotton enters the yard. With Cotton is the Sheriff, the man who has arranged the details of my death, along with several others including Chief Keeper John Kirby and the same man with the tall hat who was at the Burial Service yesterday. Though it is perhaps my imagination, it seems that of all the condemned prisoners about to die, both his and Kirby's attention is riveted on me.

Our guards unlock our feet and hands. I rub my wrists. I'm grateful to be relieved of the heavy iron circlets but scared out of my wits.

"Pinion them," says the Sheriff. At the command, guards approach with leather straps. One lashes my hands while another secures a leather strap tightly around my body, pinning my arms to my sides.

Behind me, Patrick Danville's sobs grow louder, and Owen

Haggarty screams loudly. He must be fighting the guards once more judging by the sound of cursing and the familiar thud of a truncheon connecting on his body.

"Only enough room on the gallows for six at a time." The Sheriff looks at us all as if he were picking cows at an auction. "That lot over there," he says to the guard. "They can meet their end first."

Mary and I have been selected to hang first, and I feel my knees buckle when the Sheriff's finger points at me. The boy Patrick Danville is among us, weeping piteously. "I'm sorry, I'm sorry! Mercy! Ma! Help me!" he sobs but his pleas fall on deaf ears. He will find no mercy at Newgate.

A white nightcap is placed on my head, and, with the sheriff and Ordinary Cotton leading our strange progression, we march towards the large iron portcullis.

"Be strong," says Mary. "All you've got left is your dignity, Libby. They've taken everythin' else; don't you let them take that from you, too."

The Debtor's Door opens and the crowd in the square erupts: five hundred, a thousand people or more, shouting, booing, cheering: a cacophony of noise that hits my ears as we step through the door, walk up a flight of wooden steps and onto the gallows.

"See 'em up there?" says Mary. There are several dozen people leaning out of prison windows, some with bottles of wine in their hands even at this early hour. "Them's the ones who came to the chapel yesterday. I wager they paid ten pounds for the view, all of it goin' into John Kirby's silken pocket."

The bulk of the large crowd does not have such expansive sightlines. They are pressed together on the ground, held back from the gallows by a wooden railing and a dozen uniformed soldiers with pikes — long, wicked-looking spears that could run a person through with ease.

The gallows is a large, wooden platform with a horizontal beam, braced up by two posts at either end. Six hemp ropes, a wicked-looking noose at the end of each, dangle down from the beam.

A nondescript middle-aged man stands on the platform besides a lever, waiting patiently for us to arrive. An open, horse-drawn cart sits beside the gallows, six wooden caskets piled up in the back. I can't help wondering which one is for me.

"That bloke is Mr. William Brunskill, the executioner of Newgate," Mary says. "I've seen 'im do his work a time or two from in the mob. It's a great place to pick a pocket or cut a purse, what with everyone's attention on the condemned. He'll pull these caps down over our faces, put the nooses 'round our necks, then wait for Reverend Cotton to say a final prayer. After that? Brunksill will pull back that lever, the trap door will fly open and down we drop, off to see the Almighty."

"I dinnae ken how ye can be so calm, Mary." I'm terrified. My legs move forward only because of the guard pulling me along. My head rings, and I feel dizzy, the whole world spinning around me like a top.

"What else can I do? "Entertain the crowd by wailin' like a baby? No, Libby. This is my fate. I will accept it and 'ope the 'angman does his work proper." Mary sounds both sad and bitter at her fate.

"What do ye mean by 'proper'?"

"Brunskill's good enough at his job but sometimes necks don' break from the drop," says Mary. "Then prisoners dangle for a while, alive, chokin' slowly. You can't see 'em, but I'd wager Brunskill has some 'elpers under the gallows, all set to grab 'old of our legs and pull, to 'elp us along if needed."

The sheriff motions to the executioner. "This is it, Libby," says Mary. Her voice is now trembling. Resigned to her fate or not, the terror of this day has finally gotten to her.

Under Brunskill's orders, we are lined up underneath the nooses. From behind, a guard pulls down my nightcap. Things go black. My breath comes in ragged gasps, my body shakes uncontrollably as the rough hemp noose is slipped over my neck then tightened around my throat.

I can't see, but in the few seconds I have left, my hearing seems to have been heightened, every word spoken by the multitude easily distinguished. Suddenly I think of Clara and wonder if she stood in the exact same place I do now.

"Hats off in front!" I hear someone in the crowd cry. "I can't see!"

"Get on with it!" yells another.

"Save my son! Please! Patrick's only fourteen! He's just a little boy!" a woman calls, though her pleas for clemency are met with catcalls and jeers.

"May the Lord have mercy on your souls," Reverend Cotton pronounces, concluding the Last Rites.

I clench my eyes. I know I will never see Duncan again but at least he's alive. I try to find some solace that in just a few seconds I will see both Clara and my parents.

A hush falls over the crowd. Brunskill must be about to move the lever. My heart climbs into my throat. I brace my legs for the floor to open beneath me, for the sudden drop and the jerked stop that will, if I'm lucky, break my neck cleanly. Any second. Any second the wood beneath my feet will be replaced by empty air.

I take a breath, my last I'm certain. "Godspeed, Libby," weeps Mary gently. "Godspeed."

"Hold," a firm voice says.

Mutters of confusion and surprise rise from the crowd. I hear footsteps then feel hands on my neck, hands that loosen the noose and, with my face still covered by the nightcap, hands that pull me away from the gallows.

Surprise gives way to outrage as the assembled horde voices their displeasure. Keys jingle and a door, the Debtor's Door I can only imagine in my confused, befuddled state, creaks open. "Carry on," the voice says again.

The Debtor's Door slams shut, but before it does I hear the crowd cheer as the trap door crashes open. Ropes snap taut and someone screams, a terrible gurgling cry as they flail wildly about, no doubt dancing like a terrible marionette on its string.

It's a woman's voice. Mary's last wish of a clean death has been denied her, and though I am soon back in my familiar cell in Newgate, wondering why I've been spared, I know I will hear Mary's cries echo in my head for the rest of my days — however few they might be.

Chapter 19

∽

THE DOOR OF MY cell creaks open. "Hello, missy. Surprised to see me, ain't ya?"

"Leave me alone, Hobbes," I say when I see the familiar face of the gaoler in the light of the lantern he carries. I'm inviting trouble I know with my tone, but I simply cannot help it.

I have no idea how long I've been back in the condemned cell. Three days at least, though probably more. All that time I have been haunted by the sound of Mary's dying voice, by the sight of the coffins, the gallows and the others who did not escape the hangman.

"And are you surprised to see me?" Instead of Hobbes, the

fat form of Sir Cecil Hamilton steps unexpectedly into my cell.

Hobbes hangs the lantern on a hook. "Like I told you, before, girl; there's things worse than death in Newgate. I reckon you're about to discover another one o' them."

"The turnkey's right," Sir Cecil says. "I'm not going to kill you; I've just come to collect the debt you owe me."

I dinnae owe ye a thing," I cry, shrinking back into the corner. "Yer lies condemned me to death!" I'm sick to the very core to see this awful man once more.

Hamilton takes off his jacket. "Oh, but you do, my dear. "I wanted you dead, swinging from the gibbet like the scum you are, but somebody in authority ordered your pathetic life be saved for some reason, so Sir Simon Le Blanc commuted your death sentence."

Hamilton steps forward, an odd smile on his face. "Your miserable life may have been spared, but I still mean to exact some measure of vengeance and pleasure."

"Enjoy your company, missy!" Hobbes laughs, shutting the door, leaving me alone with Hamilton. I edge to the far back wall of the cell, my back pressed firmly against the damp stones.

Hamilton walks forward. He is a large man, much bigger than I am. He presses his bulk against me, pinning me to the stones. Hamilton's fingers clench into a hammy fist that he holds in front of my face. My eyes are riveted on a thick golden signet ring on the pudgy little finger of his right hand, a ring with what looks like an oak tree embossed on it, surrounded by small red stones. I know I will never forget the sight of it. "Like I said, girl. You owe me a debt."

The ring, his finger and the rest of his fist speeds towards my face. He hits me, and stars explode in my eyes. "Now let me show you how you are going to pay it."

Chapter 20

TWO WEEKS AFTER Hamilton's visit, my face is still covered with bruises. A round scar has formed on my cheek, an injury no doubt caused by the ring Hamilton wore. My lips are scabbed as well, and my entire body aches from his assault.

It is then my unexpected guest arrives. Short of the daily torment of Hobbes's visits, I have had no other company, nor an explanation why I was saved from the hangman's noose until the door suddenly swings open.

"Elizabeth, may I come in?" To my great surprise I hear a woman's voice. "My name is Elizabeth, too, Elizabeth Fry. I've been trying to see you since you arrived at Newgate, but the prisons have been closed to visitors because of typhus, at least that's what Kirby said, though I don't believe a word of it."

Hobbes looks in from the doorway, lantern in hand. "You mind your manners," he says to the woman called Elizabeth Fry. "Mr. Kirby don't need no disrespect from the likes o' you."

In the pale light of the lantern Elizabeth Fry sees my bruised body for the first time. "You poor, poor dear!" she cries, pushing her way past Hobbes. "Get out of my way, you brute! Who did this to her? Was it you? You mark my words: should anyone else lay another hand on this girl, I'll bring the full weight of the law down upon you."

Hobbes stays put. "She fell, that's what happened. Besides, I am the law 'ere! You've no power over me! This brat's nothin' but a convicted criminal."

Fury rises in Mrs. Fry's voice. "You sir, are a criminal as well as a liar! In case you don't know it, Alfred Hobbes, I have friends in the House of Commons and I promise that you'll be held personally responsible if any more harm comes to this girl."

Hobbes blanches at the use of his full name. Mrs. Fry is a slight woman and he towers over her, but there is no doubt who is in charge now. The gaoler mumbles something unintelligible under his breath, then leaves, closing the cell door behind him.

"My dear," Elizabeth Fry says gently. "I'm here. You'll be all right; no one will hurt you again, I swear it."

She stays with me all that day, and returns for the next three after that, bringing food and warm blankets when she does. When I tell her what happened to me, she cries in indignation and anger. "You have been very kind to me, Mrs. Fry. I cannae thank ye enough," I say.

Elizabeth Fry looks almost embarrassed when she speaks. "You owe me no gratitude," she says. "In fact, I believe it is I who owe you an apology."

"Whatever for?" I wonder if I'm still suffering the effects of Hamilton's beating because I can't make any sense out of what she is saying.

"I intervened in your case," Mrs. Fry says. "What I told that dreadful gaoler the other day was true; I do have well-connected friends in Parliament. Before I even met you, I beseeched them to spare your life and, thank goodness, they did. It would seem, unfortunately, that Sir Cecil was angered enough by that decision to come and exact some misplaced revenge himself."

Somebody in authority ordered your pathetic life be saved for some reason, so Sir Simon Le Blanc commuted your death sentence.

That was what Hamilton told me. Now I understand why I am still alive. Elizabeth Fry saved my life. Then I remember the horrible sound of Mary Barrington's final seconds and shudder. Without my new friend I would have died beside her.

"'Tis I who owe ye, Mrs. Fry," I say. "Without yer help I'd

be dead and in the ground. I'll exchange a few bruises for that fate any day. But why?" I ask. "What's so special about me that ye'd do such a thing."

Mrs. Fry's expression turns serious. "Libby, the fire that killed your parents took more than one hundred other innocent lives. The Hamilton Mill Inferno as it's been called was one of the worst tragedies to ever befall Glasgow."

"It was truly awful," I tell her, the memory of that day coming back to me.

"Indeed, it was," Mrs. Fry says. "Sir Cecil Hamilton was disliked by many in the city before the mill burned down. He was a man who got rich off the backs of the poor and cared little for their well-being. Now? He's the most hated man in Scotland."

"'Tis the least he deserves," I say. "I only wish Duncan had knocked his brains out that day."

Elizabeth Fry holds my hand as she speaks. "Your brother, poor brave lad he was, became a hero when he attacked Sir Cecil in such a public way. For too long the rich have taken advantage of the poor in this kingdom. The fire, your brother's courage, and his tragic death have become symbols for those who seek change in how we treat the common worker."

Mrs. Fry is kind and has saved my life, but even then, I cannot share with her Duncan's secret. The only way my brother is truly safe is if everyone in England believes he drowned when the *Leopard* went down.

"And you have become something of a *cause célèbre* yourself, Libby. Especially since your trial and last-minute reprieve on the gallows."

"A what?" I've not heard that expression before.

"It's French, it means famous case. Your name is on many people's lips these days. There is a great deal of sympathy in the country for you."

"Me?" That anyone knows my name is very surprising.

Mrs. Fry beams. "You are a very brave young lady, Elizabeth Scott, and though you may not realize it, your name has become somewhat of a rallying cry. Progressive minds in the Parliament are not only ready to look at how we treat workers in our mills and factories, but how awful and unjust our legal system is. Change is possible, in part because of you."

"When shall I be set free?" Elizabeth Fry's talk of *reform, change* and *symbols* mean little to me. All I want to know is when I can get out of prison.

"I'm not sure," Elizabeth Fry says. "I've asked John Kirby, the Chief Keeper of Newgate the same thing, but all I get is stonewalling and obfuscation, something about *reviewing your verdict, judicial processes* and other such mumbo-jumbo."

"What yer saying is that while my life has been saved, I'm still stuck here until goodness knows when." I suddenly feel quite dejected.

"I'm afraid so," Mrs. Fry says. "Still, you should count your blessings; a reprieve from the very gallows is a rare thing. I promise you, Libby Scott, that I shall use the opportunity to press your case at the highest levels until you are a free woman."

Chapter 21

"THERE'S A CHANGE OF scenery comin' for you," Hobbes says as he unlocks my cell. "These luxurious accommodations are reserved for the condemned, and since you some'ow managed to slip your neck out of the noose, you get to move. Must make room for the next lot of danglers, if you know what I mean."

I barely have time to grab my blankets before Hobbes escorts me out of the cell. "Where are ye taking me?" I ask as Hobbes leads me down a dark stone corridor, rows of iron doors on either side illuminated by the faint light of his torch as we pass.

"Don't speak till spoken to," he says menacingly. "You've

forgotten your lessons. Good thing for you that shrew of a Quaker has got 'er eye on you or I'd teach you one 'ere and now." Without speaking another word, Hobbes guides me through a warren of corridors. We travel through the maze for several moments before arriving at a large wooden door guarded by two turnkeys.

"Here she is, lads," Hobbes snickers. "Our most famous guest."

"Stand still, missy," says one of them, a wiry fellow with a scruffy beard and eyes that remind me of a rat. In his hand is an ugly set of shackles, held together with a short length of thick chain. He bends down and clamps the heavy iron bracelets around each ankle.

"Right, then, says the guard, "now that you've got on the proper jewelry, it's time to introduce you to the ladies in the Female Quarter."

The other guard opens the door. When he does, a loud chorus of talking, laughing and shouting along with the stench of unwashed bodies and full chamber pots sweeps over me. He grins when he sees me grimace. "Ain't the prettiest of smells that's for sure," he says. "That's what happens when two hundred of the nastiest women criminals in the country get locked up together. This here section is for felons. Debtors are locked up across the way."

There aren't just women in the large room in front of me. Women of all ages to be sure, but there are dozens of boys and girls as well. Some seem to be about my age while much younger ones scamper about, wearing little more than rags wrapped around their bodies. There are babies as well, crawling upon the straw-covered floor or crying in their mothers' arms.

"Cut-purses, thieves, trollops and murderers the lot o' them," says Hobbes as he pulls me into the Female Quarter. "I'm sure you'll feel right at 'ome."

I walk into the Female Quarter accompanied by Hobbes and the two guards, my chains jangling on the stone floor as I shuffle, one foot in front of the other, into the most horrible place I've ever seen in my life.

Many in the Female Quarter ignore me. Some are playing cards, others lounge about, drinking from tin cups. Two women are fighting. They throw punches at each other, all the while shouting and screaming the vilest of words. Instead of stopping them, I see two other turnkeys laughing and egging them on.

"Hello, lovely girl!" an old woman with stringy grey hair cackles at me before turning to Hobbes. "Easement of irons?" she says, pointing to her spindly legs. "Take them chains off, I beg you!"

"Get away from me, Mad Dorothy," Hobbes says unkindly. I'm confused about her request. The woman doesn't have irons on her legs after all.

"How about a kiss then?" The woman called Mad Dorothy grins at Hobbes, a horrid grimace that displays a mouthful of rotten black teeth. Between the two of them I'm not sure who has the foulest look.

"I wouldn't kiss you for all the tea in China, you old crone. Now clear off or else. You've been 'ere long enough to know what happens if you forget your lessons."

Mad Dorothy shuffles away. "A kiss! A kiss!" she cackles.

Slightly above eye level is a series of small iron grates. At each one a woman stands, her hands stuck out between the bars. "Penny for a poor woman to buy food for her lad?" one cries.

"Who's she talking to?" I ask Hobbes.

"Beggin' from some bloke on the street for money, no doubt," he replies. "Nothing's for free in Newgate."

"'Nothing's fer free?' You have to pay to be here?" I'm not quite sure what Hobbes means. This is prison after all. No one has a choice to be here.

"Convicts get bread and water courtesy of the prison," Hobbes tells me as we walk deeper inside the Female Quarter. "Enough to keep 'em alive. Everythin' else comes at a cost. You want the shackles off your legs? That's a shillin'. Nice piece of lamb, carrots or potatoes? A few pence for each. You want blankets, books, gin, tobacco, clothes, a visit from your mum? You can get anything you want — but it all comes with a price."

"How on earth can someone get money in here?" I cannot believe what I'm hearing this loathsome man say.

"Ask friends and family if you 'ave some," Hobbes says. "Beggin' like that lot over there is another option." Then Hobbes leans over and leers at me, the smell of his breath as bad as it ever was. "And you can earn a few coppers if you're *nice* to us turnkeys, if you know what I'm talkin' about." I shudder as Hobbes speaks. There are only a few things he could be talking about, and all are disgusting.

"You're not likely to have to worry about money, though. That Mrs. Fry woman's adopted you as 'er pet. No doubt she'll 'ave you eatin' roast beef and Yorkshire puddin' when she finds out you've been moved to the Female Quarters."

Elizabeth Fry. I had forgotten all about her in the shock of moving from my old cell. I take a grateful breath; there is no doubt she will help me when she finds out what's happened.

"Of course," Hobbes continues, his face breaking into a gruesome leer. "Typhus, cholera, a knife in the back as you sleep; life can be short in Newgate, even in the Female Quarter. You may not be around when she makes 'er way back."

"At least I won't have to see yer face," I tell him. Hobbes is a loathsome man but with his name known to Elizabeth Fry I know he can't hurt me. Besides, Hobbes works the condemned cells not the Female Quarters, and if there is one small advantage in moving here, it is that I will be free of him.

"Oh no, missy," he says gleefully. "That's where you're wrong. You're a troublesome little thing, and Mr. Kirby hisself ordered me transferred to the Female Quarter to keep an eye on you. We're gonna be spendin' a lot more time together after all."

Chapter 22

⌒

"MRS. FRY! Thank goodness yer back!" It has been a week since I was moved, and all the while I've waited desperately for my new friend to return to Newgate. At least I think it's a week. The days in the Female Quarter are long and horrible and dark.

"Had I only known that unspeakable man Kirby had sent you to the Female Quarter, I would have been back the very next day. How are you?"

"Oh, Mrs. Fry," I begin. Ages ago Clara warned me about crying. She urged me to be brave and strong, but now I break down and weep, collapsing into her arms. *How am I?* I am cold, hungry, sore from the hard floor and the chains that rub on my ankles. But even more than that I am completely without hope.

"Guard!" Elizabeth Fry shouts.

"What do you want?" Hobbes asks, his face as sour as ever.

"Easement of her irons for a start, Alfred Hobbes," Mrs. Fry says, tossing the man a small silver coin.

"Well then, consider it done." Hobbes grins as he tucks the coin into his pocket. Hobbes then slips a large iron key into the locks. I feel their weight fall away and though I know it is nothing but an illusion, it seems as if I am now light enough to float into the air and out of Newgate prison.

"What else can I do for you, Libby?"

"Perhaps some food?" I ask.

"Of course, you must be famished, you poor thing. When was the last time you ate?"

"Yesterday, I think. For those prisoners without money or family visiting them in the Female Quarter, the guards distribute chunks of bread, although it is stale and seems as hard as an iron bar."

"I have just the thing." Elizabeth Fry has brought with her a satchel. "Cheese, fresh bread, some cold roast beef and a fresh apple," she says. "Does that sound all right to you?"

"It sounds like the finest meal I've ever eaten," I tell her. I take a bite of the cheese. It is rich and sharp and delicious, and I am about to gobble the rest of it down when I look behind Elizabeth and see a small boy, four years old at most, staring hungrily at the food.

"Come here, lad," I tell the boy. He is so thin I can see his ribs poking out of his skin. He has no shoes, and wears nothing save an old tattered shirt far too large for him.

Like a frightened animal, he edges closer, hand stretched out as I offer him cheese and a morsel of roast beef. He snatches both then retreats to a corner, eating the food as quickly as he can.

"Mrs. Fry, I cannae eat when these wee bairns are so hungry. Give whatever else you've brought to them."

We are surrounded now by two dozen children of various ages, all thin and sallow, all desperate for food. "You are a very kind and brave young lady. You! Hobbes," she says reaching into her bag. "Here's two crowns. Take them to Smithfield market and buy as much fresh bread and cheese and apples as you can with it. These children need to eat."

"And what's in it for me?" Hobbes asks suspiciously.

"Another shilling on your return if you do the job properly," she tells him. "And don't try to cheat me, Alfred Hobbes. I know the cost of a bushel of apples or a round of cheese, and if you come back one slice of bread short, it will be the last time you ever get money from me."

"Fair enough," Hobbes says as Mrs. Fry passes him the large silver coins. "I should be back in half an hour. You'd best have that shillin' ready for me."

"What about me, miss? Not all of us here have friends and family on the outside. I can't remember the last time I had a piece of apple." The question comes from a woman who approaches us. She looks to be about my mother's age when she died. She's gaunt and sickly-looking, with short brown hair and a filthy dress.

"Give her what you brought for me," I tell Elizabeth. "She needs it more than I do. Your name is Polly, isn't it?" I've not been here long and there are many women and children locked up in the Female Quarter, but I've started to recognize names and faces.

"Aye, Polly Snell's my name," she says, gratefully taking the food Mrs. Fry offers her. "God bless you, miss."

"Why are you in Newgate, Polly?" Mrs. Fry asks.

"You really want to know?" Polly seems surprised that anyone would take an interest in her.

"I do," Mrs. Fry replies. "I'm quite concerned about the fate and the treatment of women prisoners."

Polly almost seems embarrassed when she answers. "I was hungry, but I didn't have no money, so I pinched some bacon in Greenwich Market. I'm here for five years because of it."

"Five years fer stealing bacon?" I can't believe what I'm hearing. "Ye must have taken an entire pig."

Polly shakes her head as she eats the apple. "Two pieces."

Elizabeth Fry is incredulous. "You've been sentenced to five years in gaol for stealing two rashers of bacon?"

"At first I was to be transported but the judge decided to show me mercy."

"Some mercy," Elizabeth Fry says. "Something must be done about the laws that send poor women and children to this terrible place."

"Mrs. Fry," I ask, "thank ye so much fer the food, but I was wondering if ye'd be able to get something else for me?"

"Of course, Libby. What do you need?"

"One of the worst things about this place is the monotony. There is simply nothing to do, nothing to distract my mind, and the boredom is numbing my mind. A book, perhaps?" I say. "Something I can read to take my mind off this place?"

Mrs. Fry seems shocked at my request. "You can read? How on earth did a crofter girl from the Highlands learn how to read?"

"Back in Loch Tay my mother taught me, though my father thought it a waste of time."

"Of course I can bring you a book, Libby," Mrs. Fry says. "And I think I have just the thing."

Chapter 23

ELIZABETH FRY'S ARRIVAL back in the Female Quarter is greeted by smiles and cheers by both the women and children who live in this terrible place. The food she'd sent Hobbes out to get arrived within the hour. In fact Hobbes needed the help of the other guards to carry in all the apples, ham, bread, cheese and cakes — enough for everyone in the Female Quarter to eat.

"This must have cost you a fortune!" I say.

"My family does well enough," she says, almost embarrassed to admit it. "We have interests in banking, tea and chocolate, of all things, and it is our duty to help those less fortunate than ourselves. Our business interests extend to the Continent, the United States and the colonies of Canada."

"Thank you, miss", or "God bless you, miss," the women say, one after the other when they receive their portions.

The only person in the Female Quarter with a sour look on his face is Hobbes. "I don' know why you bother feedin' this rabble," he says. "Thieves and cutpurses the lot o' them."

"No, Mr. Hobbes," she replies curtly. "They are poor women who have had to resort to desperate measures to save themselves and their children. If I can give them comfort and sustenance, then that is what I will do until this entire rotten system is fixed."

"Suit yourself," Hobbes sniffs, "but I wouldn't waste a single copper on any of 'em in 'ere."

Mrs. Fry turns her attention to me once the prisoners have been fed and Hobbes has shuffled away. "I have something for you as well," she says.

"A book?"

"A book indeed. One of my favourites." The book is a small, leather-bound volume. "*Gulliver's Travels*. Have you heard of it? It was written by a man named Jonathan Swift."

"Nae," I reply. "What's it about?"

"That is a very good question," Mrs. Fry says. "On the surface it's about a man named Lemuel Gulliver who has a series of remarkable adventures in a country called Lilliput, amongst other places, but it has a deeper meaning as well."

"Like what?" I'm curious to learn that a book could mean two things at once.

"Perhaps you will discover that for yourself when you read it," she says. "Books can hold many secrets."

Along with the book, Elizabeth Fry gives me pencils, a small pen knife to sharpen them and several sheets of paper. "Do you like to draw? I thought they would help you pass the time."

"Aye, though I have naught had much chance to use fancy pencils and paper. Charcoal from the fireplace and a piece of dry wood or a scrap of cloth is what I'm used to." I smile at the memory. It's the first time I've thought about such things for a very long time. "I used to like drawing pictures of our cows," I say. "I loved our cows."

Mrs. Fry smiles at my story. "So, you're an artist as well as a reader! Did you get that from your father?"

"Goodness, nae. My father had no time for such silly notions. My mother was the artist; she could make an embroidery seem as real as if ye were peering out the window."

My mother. I've not thought of her or my father for an age either. Suddenly thoughts of our last day in Glasgow flood into my mind. I remember their faces when they kissed Duncan and me goodbye. I remember the fire and the grief. I remember Sir Cecil hitting me and Duncan coming to my rescue, and I remember taking the tapestry my mother made of our old home in Loch Tay off the wall and giving it to Duncan.

Take it, I told Duncan. *'Tis all we have left of them now.*

"Libby, are you all right? You look like you've seen a ghost!"

"I'm fine," I say. "Just thinking about my family. 'Tis been a while since I've done that."

"You are a very brave young woman, Libby," Mrs. Fry says hugging me.

"I dinnae think I'm brave. I'm just a prisoner."

"Bravery comes in all shapes and sizes, Libby," she tells me. "You are as brave no doubt as your brother was, rest his soul."

Duncan.

I've been thinking a great deal about my brother of late as well. Perhaps it was Elizabeth's mention of Canada. I want desperately to ask her to see if there is anything she can do to help find Duncan. But then I remember the treachery of Tinker and the crippled sailor Will back on the Liverpool docks. I like Elizabeth Fry very much, but I've learned from painful experience that sometimes those you trust the most are the first to betray you. Perhaps one day I shall share my secret with Elizabeth Fry, but that day is not today.

Chapter 24

"WHAT ARE YOU DOIN'?" Hobbes asks.

"Drawing," I reply.

"Drawin' what? Let's 'ave a look."

Hobbes walks over, swaying slightly. He's earned several shillings recently and by the looks of him he's spent the money on gin or ale.

"Our farm at Loch Tay." Hobbes takes the picture from my hand, my nose wrinkling when I smell his breath. Gin, most definitely gin. Many of the women in here have a taste for it as well. It breaks my heart to see them resorting to such awful stuff to ease their pain, but who am I to judge? I've been in the Female Quarter for only a week while many have been here ten years or more.

"What's this?" Hobbes jabs his dirty finger at an object in the picture.

"Our old cow," I say. Elizabeth Fry was teasing when she said I should draw her, but I thought it was a good idea, although bringing up the memories was hard.

"Cow?" Hobbes slurs, chuckling loudly. "Looks more like a large dog! An ugly one at that!"

"Don't ye have something else to do?" My reply is curt, but I'm not scared of Hobbes anymore. With Mrs. Fry looking after me he knows better than to hurt me.

"You mind your manners, missy," he growls, "else you'll be taught a lesson or two." But his threats to me are empty and we both know it.

Hobbes shuffles awkwardly away, leaving me to my work when I hear another voice. "I had a cow when I was a girl. Bessie, her name was Bessie. Bessie, Bessie, Bessie." Mad Dorothy slumps down beside me and looks at the picture with faraway eyes, all the while chanting the name of her cow, dead now forty years, no doubt. "This cow looks just like Bessie."

"Thank ye, Dorothy. 'Tis kind of ye to say that." When I first met Mad Dorothy, I was frightened of her. With her long scraggly hair and black teeth, she looked like a witch, and in truth she may be insane, though she's never hurt anyone all the while she's been in Newgate.

"Sad, isn't it? What this place does to a person." Polly Snell says, walking over to us.

"Has Dorothy really been in Newgate for forty years?"

"So they say. She's the longest serving prisoner in Newgate in any event," Polly says. "She's not said a sensible word since I've been here but some of the older ladies say that Dorothy's been here since she was your age."

"That cannae be true!" I find it impossible to believe that somebody would have spent nearly their entire life locked away here.

Polly eases herself down onto the ground and puts her arm around Dorothy, who still chatters away about her cow. "The story is that her family moved to London from the country when she a little girl. No one's quite sure what happened to her family, but Dorothy ended up on the streets picking pockets. She got caught, was sentenced to swing but she was pregnant, so she ended up here instead."

"What happened to her child?"

"No one knows for certain. Some say he was stillborn, others that he died as an infant. Still more say the boy was taken away from her and sent to a workhouse; nobody knows for sure. Anyone who was in prison with Dorothy from those days is long dead."

Polly turns to my picture which is sitting on top of *Gulliver's Travels.* "It's a good picture," she says. "I can see why Dorothy likes it."

"Thank ye, I'm not the greatest of artists but I do try."

"And a book? You can read?" Polly seems quite surprised. "May I see it?"

"Of course you may."

Polly flips open the book and stares at the letters. "I don't see nothing but little snakes and squiggles on the paper. Good on you for making any sense of it. What's it called?"

"My mother showed me how to read. The book is called *Gulliver's Travels*. It's about a sailor who has strange adventures."

"Lucky for you," Polly says. "I never knew my mother."

"Oh boo 'oo! Nobody feels sorry for a miserable thief like you. Your mother died 'o shame at the sight of you, most likely."

I cringe. Hobbes has returned, a near-empty gin bottle in his hand. "Leave us alone, Hobbes."

"You watch your tongue," he says, his tone threatening, his voice thicker now with the gin than before. "That Quaker do-gooder ain't around right now to protect you. Maybe I'll teach you a lesson 'ere and now after all, like takin' your little picture and tearin' it to shreds!"

"Don't hurt my cow!" To my great surprise Mad Dorothy pulls herself up and stands between Hobbes and myself. Somehow in her addled mind she must think my picture is her real cow from years ago.

"What did you say?" At first Hobbes seemed confused that somebody would challenge him. His confusion, however, is quickly replaced by anger.

"Dorothy, it's all right. Nobody's going to hurt yer cow." I quickly get to my feet. I've seen that look on Hobbes' face before, have seen what he can do to people when he's in a rage. Elizabeth Fry's warning to Hobbes or not, there is nothing she could do now. "She's sorry," I say to Hobbes. "She didn't mean anything by it. She's not right in the head and ye ken it."

Hobbes stumbles closer, his face red, his eyes burning at Dorothy. "You dare tell me what I can do?"

"Nae, she doesn't. She's sorry; we both are." I try to calm Hobbes down but between the anger and the gin he doesn't seem to be hearing a word I'm saying.

"Don't hurt my cow!" Dorothy shouts again. This time she shuffles towards Hobbes, her fists clenched. She swings her arm, a feeble move that comes nowhere close to hitting him.

"Don't you dare!" For a man his size and despite the gin, Hobbes moved more quickly than I could imagine. I watch in horror as Hobbes smashes the gin bottle into the side of Old Dorothy's head. It connects with a sickening crunch, glass shattering. Dorothy crumples to the ground amongst the shards of broken glass. She lies there, blood streaming from her head, running in little red rivulets across the stones.

"That'll teach you!" Hobbes bellows.

"What have ye done?" I scream. I rip a corner from my skirt and press it to her head to stop the bleeding. "Dorothy! Wake up!" But Dorothy does not wake up. She remains there on the floor, eyes open staring blankly into space.

"She tried to hit me," Hobbes says as he stares down at Dorothy's limp form, the remnants of the broken bottle still in his hand. He seems confused, and stares about wildly.

"Dorothy!" Polly screams. Other women have heard the

commotion and have approached. Life in Newgate is very monotonous, so whenever something out of the ordinary happens it draws attention.

"He killed her!" I cry, pointing at Hobbes. "For no reason!" Soon, the entire Female Quarter erupts in angry cries and screams. Dorothy was half-mad, but people liked her and are furious at her tragic and senseless end. A large threatening crowd gathers around Hobbes.

"Clear off! All of you!" A dozen guards run towards us, their clubs raised.

"What the blazes did you do, Hobbes?" asks one of the guards when they see Dorothy's still form on the ground, blood pooling around her.

"I taught 'er a lesson," Hobbes says faintly, looking at Dorothy as if he can't believe what he sees.

"Get him out of here," a short guard with a drooping mustache says. I don't know his name but this one seems to be the one in charge of the guards in the Female Quarter, the way he gives orders to the others.

"Come on, Hobbes," another says. "Shift's done for the day." Hobbes walks slowly away, looking back at Dorothy as he does.

One guard, a vicious-looking fellow with a full beard approaches Polly and me. "You saw nothing, do you understand? I mean *nothing*. One word out of you about what happened here, and you'll share the same fate."

"I understand," I tell the turnkey. There is no doubt he means every word.

"And get her out of here, too," the guard barks, stepping away from me. Two others grab Dorothy by her legs and with no ceremony drag her along the stones then through the doors which are locked quickly enough behind them. Inside, there is nothing left to show poor Mad Dorothy ever lived at all, save for the trail of blood her body left behind.

"I can't believe she's gone." Polly Snell slumps down against the wall, eyes red with tears.

"Will Hobbes be arrested?"

"Arrested? Most likely he won't even be spoken to by the chief keeper. She swung at him, that's all he has to say."

"But it's murder fer goodness sake! Dorothy couldn't hurt a fly, let alone a brute like Hobbes! It's not just!" I'm sad but more than that I am so very angry at the waste of Dorothy's life. That Polly thinks Hobbes will evade justice for what he did sickens me.

"Look around you, Libby. You should know that the law won't come after Hobbes. He is the law. We were told not to say a word and even if we did who would believe us?"

I catch my breath. Polly is right, and I know it. Poor Mad Dorothy won't find any justice — at least not in Newgate. But perhaps there is another way. My picture of our old farm in Loch Tay sits on the stones, Dorothy's blood soaking the corners red. "Perhaps not here in Newgate," I say, "but I vow that someday Hobbes will pay for what he did."

Chapter 25

GULLIVER'S TRAVELS is difficult to read. I don't understand some of the words and it takes several attempts to pronounce many of the others, but I can follow the story well enough to read that Lemuel Gulliver survives a shipwreck and finds himself prisoner of a group of tiny people.

Letter after letter, word after word I read. I've not read for an age, not since I was a young girl in Loch Tay. I remember those days, sitting at the table beside my mother, learning words by candlelight, my mother patiently sitting beside me, until I knew every letter, could read and write words and sentences. Who could ever have known I would have been reading in such a place as Newgate?

I feel as exhausted as if I'd worked a full day in the fields. I turn my mind away from the book and think about the terrible fate that befell Mad Dorothy. Her sickening murder will stay with me forever. I don't know how but I know I will do my best to ensure that Hobbes is punished for it. "Justice will be served, Dorothy," I say before lying down on the floor. "I promise ye."

For the next three weeks I work my way through the book. When I'm not reading I watch the comings and goings around me. And such things they are. Some women spend their days lounging around, engaged in idle conversation. Others beg through the gates. Some drink gin until they cannot walk, gin provided by the turnkeys. The guards who patrol the Female Quarter are beasts, and take all sorts of liberties with the women, but at the very least Hobbes does not return.

A week after Dorothy's death another commotion arises. Sometime during the night, a poor child died, and two women tried to take the clothes off the dead little boy to give to their own children. The women fight like animals over the tattered shirt and trousers while the boy's mother, grief-stricken and angry beyond words, has jumped in to stop them. It is truly the most awful thing I've seen in Newgate.

I watch and remember. Life at Newgate is full of violence, death, poverty, hunger and cruelty. I am grateful beyond words that Mrs. Fry has given me *Gulliver's Travel* and my pencils and paper. Without these distractions I fear I would lose my mind.

I've been in the Female Quarter less than three weeks, and I think of poor Mad Dorothy who spent day after day, month after month, year after year here. I simply cannot fathom it.

I also wait for Elizabeth Fry, but she does not come back. One week gives way to two, then three until finally, on a day in late September, when Polly and I are talking, Elizabeth Fry returns. "I didn't forget about you, Libby", she says, hugging me tightly. "Kirby shut down the prison to visitors once again. Cholera epidemic this time, he claimed." Once again, she has brought with her food for the entire Female Quarter.

"Polly, would you mind giving the food out to the women, please?" Mrs. Fry asks.

"Of course," my friend says, quickly going about the task.

"I have news for you," Mrs. Fry says. "I'm pregnant!"

I hug her tightly. "How exciting! When are ye expecting?"

"I'm three months along. The baby's due in February."

"Are ye scared?" I can't imagine having a baby.

"Not really. This will be my fifth child. I know what's in front of me, though I must admit that childbirth is not the most comfortable experience for a woman."

"Ye have four bairns already?" In all the time we've spent together, Mrs. Fry has not said a word about her children.

"I was only twenty-one when our first daughter Kitty was born. After her came Rachel, John and William."

"How can ye spend time with us in Newgate and look after such a busy household?"

We have people who help us at home," she says, "and the work I do with the female prisoners is my duty as a Quaker."

"Do ye have any word on when I'll be allowed out of this cell?" I ask. Though I'm happy for Mrs. Fry I was hoping her news would be about me getting out of Newgate.

"I'm afraid not," she admits. "I've asked for you to be released immediately but have met nothing but resistance."

"I see." I cannot hide the disappointment in my voice. "I dinnae know how much longer I can stand it here, Mrs. Fry."

"Libby, do you notice that I call you 'Libby'? You must call me 'Elizabeth', not Mrs. Fry and please tell me what else is going on here."

"Murder, and a terrible thing it was." In hushed tones and despite the threats made to me, I tell Mrs. Fry everything that happened to poor mad Dorothy.

"How very awful," she says, the shock evident on her face. "I knew this place was terrible but killing a poor defenceless woman? I feel sick beyond words. The authorities must be told at once"

"Nae! Ye cannae say a thing! The turnkeys made it very clear what would happen to me should word leak out."

"They threatened you to keep silent?" Elizabeth seems as surprised at this piece of news as she was when I told her about Dorothy's death.

"Aye, and made no bones about what would happen to me if I opened my mouth. I shouldn't have told ye."

"Don't worry," Elizabeth reassures me. "I'll not say a word yet, though when we win your freedom we must tell the authorities about poor Dorothy and the other atrocities that occur here."

"I would like that very much," I say. "Perhaps one day someone will write a story about it like Mr. Swift wrote about Gulliver."

"It would be a grand story."

"Maybe someone would write my story as well. I've not been to sea or discovered strange lands, but I have had adventures of my own."

"You have at that," Elizabeth says. "And what a story that would be as well."

"What is to become of me now? I can't spend the rest of my life in this place, Elizabeth, I just can't."

"Now? Now I go back to work and find a way to get you out of Newgate. This is not over, Libby, not by a long shot."

Chapter 26

❦

"LET'S GO, MISSY! On your feet!" I'm jolted awake by the sound of somebody shouting. One second I'm asleep on the floor, and the next I'm being dragged away by two turnkeys.

"Leave me alone!" I cry, but the guards are having none of it as I'm hurried out of the Female Quarter, down a long narrow corridor and then pushed into a small stone cell. Without a word from the guards, the door slams shut, the lock slides and I am left alone in the darkness, too shocked to even cry.

Somehow I must have fallen asleep because I remember coming to as a small hatch in the bottom of the door slides open and a mug of water and a bowl of thin, cold soup is pushed into the cell. "Hello? What's going on? Why am I here?"

The answer to my questions is the sound of the hatch slamming shut. Goodness knows how long I have stayed here, locked up in the cell. It is dark all the time. The only light is the faint glow of a lantern that shines in through the gap between the door and the wall. I have no blanket, no bed, no company.

There is only one reason I can come up with why I've been moved from the Female Quarter in such a way, though the thought of it is too terrible to deal with. It can only be about my death sentence. Whoever ordered my life saved has changed his mind, and I am about to be hanged. For what seems like days I sit in the dark with this awful notion consuming me. I feel the noose around my neck, hear the roar of the crowd, feel the floor give way beneath me. And then the door opens.

"Up you get," a guard barks. I stand up, wobbling unsteadily on me feet at the command as he places a heavy set of irons on my legs. "Right. Let's go."

"Where are we going?" I ask. I squint my eyes as we exit the cell. The hallway is lit only by a small lantern but after being in the dark it burns my eyes as if it were the sun itself.

"Hold your tongue" is all the guard says in response.

We shuffle along the hallway then climb a long flight of stone stairs. At the top of the stairwell is a thick wooden door.

The guard stops and knocks. "She's here, sir," he says to whoever waits behind the entry.

"Come in," a voice says. The door opens to reveal an office of some sort, spacious, elegantly furnished and well-lit. The walls are lined with expensive-looking wood panelling and fine carpets cover the floor.

A familiar man sits behind a large desk.

The tall one with the beaky nose is John Kirby, Chief Keeper of Newgate Prison 'imself.

"You know who I am?" he asks.

"Yer Mr. Kirby, the Chief Keeper." This is the third time I have seen John Kirby. Mary Barrington told me who he was that day in the condemned pew. The second time I saw him was when I was standing on the gallows, seconds away from dying.

Kirby stands up. He is a tall rake of a man, with short hair and a large sharp nose. He looks down that nose as he addresses me. "You are a clever little lass, aren't you, though you'll soon find out you've been too clever for your own good."

"My laird?" If anything, I'm more confused than ever.

"Do you know what it means to be the Chief Keeper of Newgate Prison?" he asks.

"My laird, I dinnae ken the first thing about it." I try to answer his strange question as respectfully as I can.

"It means that I know everything that goes on inside these walls. Everything."

A sickening feeling rises in my gut. "I'm sorry, my laird,

but I'm not sure what ye mean?" I try to sound convincing but in truth I do know what he's referring to.

"You know exactly what I'm talking about! You were told to keep your mouth shut about the old woman. You knew what could happen to you, and yet you still insisted on telling Elizabeth Fry about the old woman."

"Nae, sir." I've never been good at lying but I must protect Elizabeth Fry.

Kirby doesn't believe a word of it. "Enough of your lies. You'd be surprised what people will do and say for a warm blanket, a decent meal — or a few years taken off a sentence for stealing bacon."

I know exactly who he is speaking about. "Polly? Polly would never —"

"Polly certainly would," he said, cutting me off. There is no such thing as loyalty in a prison, and when a person over-hears something important, if they are smart they will share that information with me."

I look defiantly at Kirby. "Nor is their justice in a prison, either."

Kirby smiles, a terrible knowing grin. "Oh, but that isn't true. You are about to face justice yourself. That blasted Mrs. Fry woman gave you a book about a sea voyage, *Gulliver's Travels*, I believe. I hope you can appreciate the irony that your misdeeds have earned you a journey of your own."

"Journey?"

"I may not be able to execute you, Elizabeth Scott, but no

one can stop me from transporting you. Your days in Newgate are over and you will never scheme with Elizabeth Fry again. A ship is setting sail from London to Botany Bay and you shall be on it. I do hope you enjoy Australia. If you manage to survive the trip, you will never leave its shores."

Chapter 27

MY WRISTS CHAINED tightly together, I join a line of men and women snaking along the dock, up the gangplank of the sailing ship *Indispensable*. I see its name on the ship and can make out that it is an old, three-masted ship creaking at its berth on the River Thames.

Some of the prisoners are stone-faced and accept their transportation with as much dignity as they can muster. Others, however, weep and wave frantically at the husbands, wives and children kept at bay on the dock, pushed back by the wall of soldiers and their bayonet-tipped flintlocks.

I search the crowd for Elizabeth Fry, but my friend is nowhere to be seen. It doesn't matter. There isn't anything she can do to help. There will be no appeal of my sentence. No last minute reprieve. "Do ye ken when we sail fer Australia?" I ask the man standing next to me. He's in his fifties and has the manner of someone highborn, unlike the rest of us waiting our turn in line

"I can't rightly say. It depends on a host of factors: the tide, the weather, the presence of French warships, the list goes on. We could leave tomorrow or six months from now. All I know for certain is that once we board this ship we're not seeing the sky until we reach Botany Bay."

"How is it ye know so much?" I ask him.

"I should. I used to be in the Royal Navy. Name's Walter. Walter Sturridge. What's yours?"

"Libby Scott."

"A pleasure to meet you, Libby, though I wish it were under different circumstances. You don't strike me as a criminal. However did you end up here?"

"Aiding and abetting a felon." The whole story is far too long to explain to him now.

"My apologies," Sturridge says. "It's not my business to ask." Sturridge is a gentleman. I can tell by how he speaks and the way he carries himself. I've never seen a man of his station in chains.

"'Tis all right, Mr. Sturridge."

"You are most gracious," he says. "And since you told me your crime, allow me to tell you mine, so we are even on that score. I embezzled from the Royal Navy in a time of war. I had gambling debts. I needed the money and the Royal Navy had more of it than I did. I didn't think they'd notice, but I was found out soon enough. I was a good civil servant but an even worse thief than I was a gambler. By all accounts I was set to swing from a yardarm at Greenwich Docks, but some old friends asked for mercy. Some mercy! I've been expelled from my own country. I will never see England again."

"Nor will I," I tell Sturridge. "I'm banished to Australia forever."

"Well then, I wager we'll have a great deal of time to get to know each other," he says as we step onto the deck and then climb down a steep ladder into the hold. "This ship can hold up to four hundred passengers by the looks of things, and I don't think there's more than two hundred of us yet, so it's my guess we'll wait for more to arrive. Until then, all we've really done is exchange Newgate for another sort of prison."

The hatch slams shut above us. "So if I were you, Libby, I'd find a nice corner of the ship and get as comfortable as I could; it may be years until we set foot on dry land again."

Chapter 28

THE BELLY OF THE prison ship is a terrible place to be. It's cold and damp on the river, and what little food the guards give us we must hide from the rats: large, evil creatures with long, scaly tails that crawl everywhere in the hold, biting us at will.

I'm soon cold, hungry, and covered with bites, so it's no surprise I fall ill. It begins with a fever a week or two after boarding *Indispensable* as we wait to set sail. My temperature rises, my head aches, and chills make my body shudder uncontrollably. I'm not the only one who suffers. Most of the others are soon ill as well.

"Ship's fever. Typhus. God help us all," moans Walter

Sturridge. My friend is covered with a rash and lies on the floor of the hold in agony. I break out as well, a horrible stain on my body that seems to spare only my hands and face.

There is nothing I can do to help Walter, the others, or even myself, as I fall in and out of consciousness, sweat pouring from my body. My mind is delirious, full of nightmarish dreams of gigantic rats crawling over me, of my parents burning alive, their features disappearing in the flames that consumed the mill.

I dream of Duncan, not safe but drowning, I hear him pleading for help as he helplessly sinks beneath the waves of the cold sea. Worst of all I see Sir Cecil Hamilton, hand raised, ready to strike. In my fevered dreams I feel the sting of his ring cutting into my face, can feel the scar he left ache with every beat of my heart.

I'm not sure how long I've been sick when my eyes slowly flutter open and I struggle to sit up, feeling light-headed and as thirsty as I was that first day in the prison wagon on the trip from Liverpool to London, many months ago now. The thirst aside, I feel better. My fever has broken, the inflammation on my skin subsided.

Others have not been so fortunate. Morning light streams into the hold from the barred hatchway, illuminating a scene of horror. A good number of the other prisoners are dead. Rats feast upon their bodies, and the smell of decay fills the tight space of the hold.

Of the few still alive, most are still in the grasp of fever.

They lie on their backs, groaning incomprehensibly. "Libby," a voice whispers behind me. Walter Sturridge leans against the wooden side of the hold, gasping for breath. "You're alive. Thank God. I thought you were dead for sure."

"Willna the soldiers aid us?" Those of us still living urgently need help or we will join the ranks of the dead as well.

"They'll not be of any help," Sturridge says, coughing all the while. "They've left. Abandoned ship as they say, more terrified of the typhus than their commanders. We are on our own."

"What will we do?" The prospect of staying in these awful conditions, of getting sick again or of dying of thirst and hunger, seems a much worse fate than the gallows.

"Over there, that hatch in the side of the hold. Do you see it?" On the side of a ship there's a small wooden square that has been nailed shut, but a thin sliver of light shines through the gap.

"That's a gun port," Sturridge says, pulling himself unsteadily to his feet. "This ship used to carry cannons. The ports have been boarded up, but the wood has shrunk, and the nails have started to pop. With a bit of luck, we can open it and you can get out."

"Nae, Walter, you mean *we* can get out."

"I'm afraid not, Libby." Sturridge's voice comes in fluid-filled coughs. "Thin though I've become, I won't be able to fit through."

Sturridge stumbles across the hold, his eyes searching for something. He bends down beside a broken water barrel, picks up a stave and returns. "I don't have much strength, my dear," he says, sliding the wooden slat into the thin crack. "You'll need to help."

Sturridge leans down on the barrel stave. I join him, pressing down as best I can. At first the gun port refuses to move, held firm by the stout nails, but slowly, reluctantly, as we press harder, the wood inches up, squeaking in protest.

"That's all it will go," Sturridge says, before a coughing fit overcomes him once more. The opening seems impossibly small, not even large enough for my head to squeeze through by the looks it.

"I cannae fit through there," I tell him, desperation rising in my chest.

"You can and you will," Sturridge says, his breath returning. "It's a bit of a drop, though," he says peering through the hole. "Can you swim?"

"Aye." In the fleeting Highland summer, Duncan and I would swim in the cold waters of Loch Tay after a long day in the fields. Then we'd lie on the rocks in the warm sun to dry off. The memories threaten to overwhelm me. I push them away, to stay focused on what must be done.

"Good," says Sturridge. "Luckily the tide's not running, or the current would be too strong to fight against. Kick off your shoes and get ready. When you hit the water, keep your head down and swim straight for the shore. Whatever you do, don't be seen," he adds. "If there are any soldiers about, the last thing you want to do is give them something to shoot at."

Chapter 29

STURRIDGE LEANS AGAINST the barrel stave, putting every ounce of his fading strength into it. The gap widens again, ever so slightly, as the wooden slat groans once more against the nails that hold it fast. I can fit my head into the narrow breach now, though the rough wood scratches deeply into my scalp.

"Keep going, Libby," Sturridge says. "I can't hold on much longer." I push into the opening and as the wood presses down on me, I feel as if a giant has my skull in his hands and is trying to crush it. The pain is almost unbearable, and I feel as if my head will explode, until suddenly I'm through.

I take a brief second to breathe, then keep going, my body

screaming in agony as my shoulders slide between the gun port and the small hatch. I exhale, making myself as thin as possible, my shoulders slipping clear of the wood as I do. I lean further out of the ship then look down.

It is a terrific distance to the river, running dark and murky against the ship below. I start to pull myself back into the hold. "It's too far! I cannae do it, Walter."

"Yes, you can," Walter says, and before I say another word, he lets go of the stave, wraps his arms around my legs, lifts me from the deck of the hold and propels me forward.

My chest clears the ship, then my waist, until I am past the tipping point. Then I am falling head first, my legs and arms thrashing wildly in the air.

I hit the river with a splash, sinking beneath the muddy surface. Frigid water fills my mouth as the current catches me. I feel myself brush against the wooden hull and I panic, my lungs burning as I struggle for the surface, fighting against the force of the river.

My head bursts free of the water, and I am coughing uncontrollably, gulping down the air as I twist onto my back. It is an effort to keep my head above the water; my dress feels as if it weighs a hundred pounds, that it will pull me back under, to the bottom and my death.

It takes all my strength to swim. The water is colder even than Liverpool Bay and it is a struggle to keep myself afloat. The foul water stinks like the toilet buckets in Newgate; the last thing on earth I want is to drink any more of it.

I drift with the current away from the *Indispensable*, moored alone on a pier on the northern bank of the River Thames. There are no soldiers about, and though dock-workers and sailors go about their business, no one spots me bobbing in the river.

I make my way to the shore, swimming slowly. When my feet hit the muddy bottom, I crawl on my hands and knees through the slimy mud up onto the riverbank beside an abandoned warehouse. Walking is treacherous on the slick bank, and I pick my way slowly towards the building, my eyes darting everywhere.

I reach the door of the warehouse exhausted, soaking wet and shaking from the cold. Still, I am cautious as I slowly pull open the door and peer into the gloom.

The place is empty, except for the pigeons that roost inside. The squeaking door has upset them, and they fly up through a hole in the roof, wings fluttering loudly in protest.

Inside, I see a large pile of burlap sacks. With my legs nearly numb and my eyes barely able to focus, I stumble towards them. All that matters now, more than food or water or clean clothes, is to get warm. Still shivering from the cold, I crawl deep within the pile of sacks, shut my eyes and, exhausted from the fever and my escape, I fall quickly asleep.

Chapter 30

LARGE COLD RAINDROPS fall through the hole in the roof as I climb out of the nest of sacks I've buried myself in. I'm still damp, and the stink of the river clings to my body and clothes, but though I'm hungry and thirsty, I feel better than I have in days.

I walk out of the warehouse into the cold air, still alert for people. The time of day confuses me. At first, I think I've only been asleep for a short time, but it was late morning when I left the ship, and now it is just a short time after sunrise, I wager, though the sun is hidden in the clouds. I must have slept through the entire day, the night, and well into the next morning.

The warehouse is one of several abandoned buildings on the riverbank. A large brick wall surrounds it, but the gate is broken and hangs rusting on its hinges. No one is about. I notice that rainwater has pooled on the top of an old metal tank beside the warehouse door. It must have frosted last night, as there is a thin skiff of ice across the water's surface. With the edge of my hand, I crack the ice, take a long drink then wash my face and hands, vainly scrubbing the stink of the Thames out of my skin.

What am I going to do next?

I know nothing of the city's geography, nor where I am. I have no family, no friends in the world, and there is only one person in a sea of a million souls I can turn to, just one I can count on to help. Someway, somehow, I must find Elizabeth Fry. I remember that she told me she was living at Plashet House in a place called Newham, somewhere in North London. The names meant nothing to me at the time, but they are certainly familiar to the old woman I meet, not ten minutes after leaving the waterfront.

"It ain't far at all, my little Scottish dearie," she tells me. The woman is selling cigars and matches to passers-by on a busy cobbled street full of horses, carts and working men. She stands next to a small coal fire burning in a metal brazier.

"This 'ere's Barking Road. It will lead you right to Newham 'igh Street. Walk north for 'alf an 'our or so, then you're there. Normally I'd ask for a tuppence or two for the information," she says, eyeing me sympathetically, "but you don't look like you've two coppers to rub together and you've not 'ad much to eat recently either, I'd wager."

"Aye," I say, my voice shaking. "I dinnae ken the last time I had a decent meal."

"Then take this," she says kindly, handing me over a small loaf of bread. "It was gonna be my tea, but you look like you need it more than me. And stand by the fire while you eat. You're freezin' by the looks of things as well as starvin'."

"Thank ye," I say, overwhelmed by the woman's kindness. I bite into the loaf, gulping down large mouthful as the heat of the burning coals slowly warms me up.

"You have family in Newham?" she asks, waiting patiently for me to finish the bread.

"Nae," I reply, "just a friend."

"Well then, when you get there I suggest you ask your friend if you can have a bath. No insult meant, my dear, but you smell as if you went swimmin' in the Thames, and you don't seem daft enough to do that!"

Chapter 31

ELIZABETH FRY'S HOUSE is a large, light-coloured mansion set in the trees, not far from Newham High Street. Her work with prisoners and the poor of London must be well-known here, because nobody seemed to find it strange that a girl with no shoes, wearing a ragged, dirty dress was asking strangers for her address. I reach the front entrance, draw my breath and knock.

"May I help you?" asks a maid when the large oak door swings open.

"I . . . I would like to speak with Mrs. Fry, please," I ask timidly. The maid looks at me, wrinkling her nose, her expression somewhere between pity and contempt.

"The missus don't see her clients at 'ome. Good day."

"Mrs. Fry! Please! It's Libby Scott!" I cry out, before the maid can shut the door on me. "I need yer help!"

"Excuse me!" the maid snaps curtly, "I told you the missus don't see —"

"Libby Scott? For goodness sake, Maggie, let her in!" The maid's angry outburst is cut off by the sound of a very familiar and welcome voice from inside the house. "Quickly now! Get her off the street and look to see she hasn't been followed!"

Elizabeth seems overjoyed to see me. Despite my terrible appearance and no doubt my smell, she hugs me tightly. She's visibly pregnant now, I can tell by the swell of her dress. "Libby! You're alive! Kirby told me you'd perished of typhus! How on earth did you find your way here?"

I tell Elizabeth my story, of how I was taken from the Female Quarter in the middle of the night, locked away by myself and placed on the ship. When I tell her how many people got sick and died and how Walter helped me escape, she breaks down in tears.

"I'm so sorry," she says repeatedly. "Kirby closed the prison down to visitors. Another outbreak of typhus claimed your life, he said, the lying cad! He even showed me your death certificate!"

"'Tis not yer fault," I say hugging her back. "Truly it wasn't."

"Kirby didn't want me to know he was going to transport you. Had I known, I would have done everything in my power to stop him. I'm so glad you escaped! You could have died or been sent to the farthest reaches of the world!"

"But I didn't," I say. "I'm free and I'm never going back to that place as long as I live."

Elizabeth beams. "No, you're not, but we will have to figure out what to do with you. Kirby will have heard about your escape from the ship. No doubt he will be sending his men to look for you. The world thinks you're dead, but he knows the truth. Kirby will be desperate to find you."

"Aye, I suppose yer right." With all my attention focused on finding Elizabeth Fry, I'd not actually realized my situation. *Out of the frying pan and into the fire*, as my mother used to say.

"We don't have to worry about Kirby now," Elizabeth reassures me. "In the meantime, let's see what we can do about getting you a decent meal and wash!"

Somewhat reluctantly, judging by the sour look on her face, the maid Maggie takes me into the kitchen and pours large kettles full of hot, steaming water into a copper bathtub. When the tub is full she brings me soap, washcloths and towels, then takes her leave.

I haven't had a hot bath in years, so long ago in fact that I can hardly remember the last time I did. Back in Loch Tay, on those rare times we'd bathe, I was fourth in the water, after my father, mother and brother took their turns. By the time I sat in the small copper tub, the water was dirty and more warm than hot, but it still felt like a luxury.

Those baths pale in comparison to soaking in this hot, clean water, stretched out until every inch of me is covered. The soap is sweet-smelling, like roses, and I cry with happiness and relief as the hot water washes over me.

With soap and cloth, I strip the dirt and the grime from my body, my nails and my hair, scrubbing so hard I feel as if I'll strip the very skin from my body. By the time I'm finished in the tub all that is left of Newgate, the *Indispensable*, and the putrid River Thames are bitter memories and the thick skiff of dirt that floats greasily on the surface of the cooling water.

"Libby, may I come in?" Elizabeth asks from behind the kitchen door.

"Aye, of course," I wrap myself in a large towel as she enters the kitchen, carrying a bundle of clothes in her arms.

She puts the clothes down on a chair. "This is an old dress of mine. It'll be a little too short for you, I'm afraid, and most likely loose in the mid-section. I used to be a little slip of a thing, but four children with another on the way by the time you're twenty-eight changes a woman's body!"

"Thank ye, Elizabeth," I say gratefully, but it still feels odd to be addressing her by her Christian name. My old dress lies in tatters on the floor, not worth washing.

"Get changed," she tells me, taking her leave, "then come out to the drawing room and I'll have Maggie make you tea and something to eat. It looks like it's been an age since you've had decent food."

Chapter 32

JOSEPH FRY, A QUIET, dignified-looking banker and tea merchant, about thirty years of age, seems somewhat surprised to find me there when he returns from work, but he is a Quaker like his wife, and he welcomes me into his home. I meet her children Kitty, Rachel, John and William, and I am thrilled that once they get over their shyness they treat me as if I were a big sister to them.

The weeks pass by. Autumn turns to winter and Christmas arrives. To my surprise the Frys hardly acknowledge it, although they do have a roast goose and give me a lovely present of new clothes.

"Every day is special to Quakers," Elizabeth says as we sit

by the fire drinking tea. "There was a time when none of us celebrated Christmas or New Year's Eve at all, but these days some do, and some don't. We are more traditional than most others of our Order, but with you staying with us for a while we thought it would be nice to do a little something special."

"In Loch Tay I celebrated Christmas, but I preferred Hogmanay. It was the most special day of the year."

"Hogmanay? I'm afraid I don't know that word."

"Scottish New Year. I loved this time of year back home," I say. "We'd play outside in the snow and, in the evenings, sing songs, eat and even though we didna have much money we'd give gifts. Then, as the clocks struck twelve, we would first foot."

"First foot? What's that, Libby?"

"'Tis a very important tradition," I say. "Right at the stroke of midnight the first person to enter the house should be a tall, dark-haired man or lad. If so, then good luck will be yers all year."

"What a quaint tradition," Elizabeth says. "Does it really work?"

"The year before we were evicted, a fierce snow storm hit our village. Few people were out and about, and the first person to cross the threshold of our house was my father, and he was fair-haired. He said not to worry about it, that it was nought but a quaint tradition as well." My eyes well up at the memory. "But look what happened to us afterwards."

Joseph Fry speaks up. "I may not be a tall man, Libby, but

I am dark-haired and I pledge I will be the first to cross our threshold tonight, so that this coming year brings you — brings us all — good luck."

By early January, a thick blanket of snow covers London, though it is quickly dappled grey and black with soot from the coal fires that fill the air with smoke. I'm grateful to be free of the convict ship, but I can't stay here forever and am starting to feel restless. I'm not allowed to go out onto the street, and even walking around Plashet House's garden is something I do only in the early morning or at night, when Elizabeth and Joseph are certain no prying eyes can see me, and that is why I'm most surprised at what she tells me that morning. "Libby, there's somebody I would very much like you to meet."

"Who?"

"Elizabeth must hear the worry in my voice. In the weeks since escaping the *Indispensable*, I've fretted over Kirby and the authorities finding me. As she said, I'm an escaped convict after all. "Don't worry, Libby," she reassures me. "I think you will be very happy to meet our guest. He's here to help you fulfill one of your wishes."

"My wishes?" I'm not sure what Elizabeth means as I meet her guest, a young man, well-dressed and carrying a leather case. "Libby Scott, it is indeed a pleasure to make your acquaintance."

"Libby, this gentleman is Mr. Benjamin Hanscomb of the

London Courier. The *Courier* is one of the largest newspapers in London."

"A pleasure to meet ye, my laird."

Hanscomb laughs. "I'm no laird, Libby. I'm merely a journalist and it is your story I'm here to write about, with your permission."

"My story?" I am still confused.

"Do you recall that day back in Newgate when we agreed that your adventures would make a grand story?" Elizabeth asks. "Mr. Hanscomb agrees. He wants to chronicle your experiences in the *Courier*."

Then I remember. Telling my story, if only to get justice for poor Mad Dorothy and the other prisoners of Newgate "Ye want to tell my story?"

"I do indeed, Libby. The *Courier* is a voice for progressive change in England. We are very much interested in sharing with the entire country the terrible things that have happened to you. The government must address the cruelty of the Bloody Code and the injustices it does to the poor and defenceless."

"Hear, hear!" says Elizabeth. "Well, Libby, are you up to it?"

I most certainly want to, but a terrible worry has been growing while Mr. Hanscomb speaks. "Won't people be angry with what I have to say? Will you not be put at risk if I speak, Elizabeth?"

"A very justifiable fear," Hanscomb says. "You needn't worry about Mrs. Fry and her husband. They are well protected in society. As for you? No doubt John Kirby will be most upset, as will some others like Sir Cecil Hamilton. Powerful men like these have been profiting from human misery for years. But, if what you say is truthful, you have nothing to fear. Besides, I will not tell anyone where you are hiding."

Perhaps Mr. Hanscomb is right, but he wasn't the one that stood on the gallows or was locked away for months. "What will they do with me if I'm found somehow? I dinnae want to go back to Newgate or be transported or hanged."

"No one will find you, Libby," Elizabeth assures me, "and you'll never go back to that awful prison again."

"Think of the good you'll be doing for those other poor women still locked up in Newgate," Hanscomb says. "Yours is the only voice they have."

Mr. Hanscomb's words ring true. I am free while others who have endured far more than I are still locked up in Newgate. Despite the risks, I know it is the right thing to do. "Then I shall use my voice to speak up for my parents, my brother, Mary Barrington, poor Mad Dorothy and even Polly Snell. What would ye like me to do, Mr. Hanscomb?"

The journalist beams as he takes out a journal and a quill pen. "Just start from the beginning."

"Very well," I say, taking a deep breath. "My name is Elizabeth Scott, though most call me Libby. I was born in Loch Tay and lived for most of my life in the Highlands, until tragedy and misfortune brought me to London, where I became a girl of Newgate Prison."

"A Girl of Newgate Prison." Hanscomb repeats my words slowly, his pen scratching across the paper. "But not just *a* girl of Newgate Prison. No Libby, you shall be *the* girl of Newgate Prison, the voice and the face for all those poor souls locked away in that horrible place. What a tremendous beginning to a story, a tremendous beginning indeed."

Chapter 33

I SPEAK TO BENJAMIN HANSCOMB for hours, stopping only when my voice starts to give way. His hand must be aching as well, judging by the way he rubs his fingers when he stops writing. We've reached the point in my story where Duncan and I have separated on the Liverpool docks, though even now I do not dare say that Duncan did not sail on the ill-fated *Leopard*.

"That wretch Tinker!" says Hanscomb. " I can't believe he would do that to you and your brother. Simply unforgivable."

"I thought that for the longest of times as well," I say. "But I've come to understand that people are just trying to survive in a cruel, terrible world. I willnae ever forget what he did, but I've forgiven him. And others as well."

"That is tremendously generous of you," Hanscomb says, putting away his book. "You must be tired and need to rest. Are you fine with me coming back tomorrow to get the rest of your tale written down?"

"Of course, Mr. Hanscomb; I'm very much looking forward to it."

Elizabeth Fry and I bid Mr. Hanscomb goodnight and have a small meal, though I can barely keep my eyes open as I eat. It's much harder opening old wounds and talking of my family than I'd have thought. When my head hits the pillow, I'm asleep before I know it.

Mr. Hanscomb returns the following day and stays for hours talking to me. We break for the day, stopping my tale just before I'm sent to the *Indispensable* for what I'd assumed would be my voyage to Australia.

"You did great work today, Libby," Mr. Hanscomb says. "I shall return tomorrow morning to finish things up if that's fine with you?"

"'Tis my pleasure." And in truth it is. Telling my story is very tiring but it somehow feels as if I'm cleansing my heart as well.

By the end of the next day I've finished.

"I cannot thank you enough for this, Libby. It is truly a remarkable account and I know our readers will be captivated," Hanscomb says.

"And more than that," adds Elizabeth Fry, "the public outrage will no doubt put pressure on our leaders to finally reform our rotten system. When will your story be published, Benjamin? I'm most excited to see it in print."

"As am I, Mrs. Fry. The *Courier* intends to serialize Libby's story. Every Saturday for the next four weeks we will publish a portion. The typesetters at the paper are preparing for our Saturday edition as we speak."

"And your publishers have agreed to my request?" Elizabeth asks, though I'm not certain what request she is talking about.

"They have indeed," Hanscomb says. "Quite happily so, I am pleased to say."

"Excellent. Then good day to you, sir! Both Libby and I can't wait to see the Saturday paper!"

"Thank ye, Mr. Hanscomb," I say as the writer is leaving the house.

"No, thank you, Libby," he replies. "You are indeed a remarkable young lady."

"What request did ye make of the newspaper?" I ask Elizabeth once the door has closed behind Benjamin Hanscomb.

"I will tell you in due course," she says. "Suffice it to say that it is one I asked for with your best interests in mind."

Elizabeth speaks no more of whatever request she has made, and I quickly forget about it. I've asked her to give me chores to do around Plashet House. She has been very generous in allowing me to stay with her, and I won't take advantage of her kindness. I like to keep busy and am more than happy to help. I particularly like spending time with her children. I play with them all, and I soon feel as if I'm really like an older sister. Friday passes by slowly and despite my comfortable bed in the room I share with Rachel and Kitty, it's difficult to fall asleep with the anticipation of the paper's arrival.

Somehow I manage to drift off to sleep. Usually I'm one of the first in the house to wake up, but for whatever reason I stay fast asleep in the morning until I'm woken up by Elizabeth's excited voice. "Libby! Get up! You must come and see!"

Then I remember. "The paper? It's here?"

"It is! Joseph picked up several copies this morning!"

I climb out of bed, throw on a dressing robe, and follow Elizabeth downstairs to the drawing room. "A remarkable account," says Joseph Fry. He is sitting in his chair reading the paper when we enter. "Well done, young lady."

He passes me my own copy. "It begins on page three."

I flip open the paper and sure enough, in thick black letters I see *The Girl of Newgate Prison* at the top of the page. "My name is Elizabeth Scott," it begins, just as I said to Mr. Hanscomb, "though most call me Libby."

"Word for word!" I exclaim. "Every word I said is here! Each and every one!"

"And what words they are, Libby Scott," says Elizabeth. "And we shall soon see the power they have to change England for the better."

Chapter 34

EACH SATURDAY THAT follows brings with it the next segment of my story. I am pleased to see that Mr. Hanscomb has faithfully recorded my words, though when I read, I find it hard to believe that these things have happened to me, and that they are not from some sort of story book. Part of me feels very much like Lemuel Gulliver himself.

"I have to tell you as well that the *Courier* has generated a significant amount of attention across the country because of your account," says Elizabeth on the day the last section of my story was published. "And why would it not? *'And with my heart heavy for poor brave Walter Sturridge, I strode upon the shore, turned my back on London and all the horrors it brought me and walked away to freedom.*'" Elizabeth puts down the paper and sighs. "What a beautiful way to end your tale."

"Well it's not like we can tell people I'm tucked away in yer house in Newham," I say.

"True," Mrs. Fry agrees, "Besides, it gives your story a certain mystery, don't you think? You are the talk of the town and you have struck a fine blow for reform. Men of influence across the city are reading and paying attention."

Before Elizabeth can say another word, the door chime rings. "Who on earth can that be?" Elizabeth asks. We never have visitors calling this early in the morning."

I hear Maggie, Mrs. Fry's maid, answer the door and speak to whoever is there. Maggie has not warmed up to me since I arrived at Plashet House. It's not that she's rude or cruel to me but I always get the sense that somehow Maggie feels I am beneath her.

This feeling is not lessened when Maggie enters the dining room. She carries a white card in her hand and scowls at me when our eyes meet. "A gentleman is here to see you and Mrs. Fry," Maggie says. She passes Joseph Fry the card and I can see the surprise in his eyes when he reads it.

"Libby, would you mind using the back stairs and going up to your room for a moment or so?"

"Joseph?" Elizabeth sounds alarmed. "What's going on?"

"Everything will be fine," he says. "I will come and get you in a little while but now I need you to go upstairs, Libby."

"Aye, Mr. Fry," I say. Despite his assurance to the contrary,

I can't help feeling that things most certainly are not fine. Still, I do as I'm told and return to my room where I sit anxiously and wait for an explanation.

Kitty is sitting on her bed, playing with a little doll. "What's going on, Libby? You don't look well."

"I'm fine," I say. "A wee bit under the weather is all." I don't want Kitty to worry about me, and so I while away the time playing with her. It is not until some time has passed that I hear footsteps in the hallway.

"Libby, please come back down. I have something to tell you, something very important." I hear Elizabeth call my name from down the stairs.

"Aye, what is it?" I ask as I return to the sitting room, curious to know just who has come to the house.

"Your story has caused quite the commotion in Parliament as well, it seems. There are some who are demanding the arrest of both John Kirby and Sir Cecil Hamilton, and there are calls for that repulsive turnkey Alfred Hobbes to face justice for the murder of that old woman, to hang even, from the Newgate gallows itself."

"I want justice for Mary, Clara, Mad Dorothy and fer my family, but I don't want anyone, even Hobbes, to die because of what I said."

"There's more," Mrs. Fry adds. There are also those who are very angry with Mr. Hanscomb and the London *Courier* and want *them* to face severe punishment, not Sir Cecil or John Kirby."

"Mr. Hanscomb?" I'm shocked at the news. "He's done naught wrong. 'Tis I who told the story."

"Perhaps, but Mr. Hanscomb is the one who wrote that a Newgate turnkey murdered a prisoner and that Sir Cecil assaulted you in the prison. Hamilton and Kirby deny both things happened. They are but two of the powerful people who profit from the misery of our justice system and who have everything to lose if your claims are proven true," Joseph Fry says, looking up from his coffee.

"So that man came to the house today? To tell you all this?"

"In part. Our visitor is the private secretary of Baron Hawkesbury. He brought with him a message from his employer."

"Baron Hawkesbury? I dinnae ken who that is."

"Baron Hawkesbury is the Home Secretary, Libby. He is one of the most important men in the country. He oversees all the institutions within the United Kingdom — including our justice system."

"Why would such a man send his secretary to see you?"

"That is the thing, isn't it?" says Joseph Fry. "Hawkesbury is a Tory. Normally a member of that party would be the first to defend the Bloody Code, but of late the Home Secretary has expressed a desire to end the slave trade and improve the lot of the working people of England, including those unfortunate enough to be incarcerated. Some even believe he is a secret reformer. In any event, Hawkesbury has an independent streak. I believe he has read your story with a sympathetic ear and that he doesn't believe what is being said about you and Mr. Hanscomb."

"What is being said about us?"

"That you died in prison, and that Mr. Hanscomb's written account is more from his imagination then your own life."

"How could anyone make up such a thing?" I am shocked that people would believe such lies."

"Easier than you think, Libby," interjects Elizabeth Fry. "Your story was well-known and published in the papers. The transport lists are publicized in the papers, including in the *Courier*, and Mr. Sturridge's embezzlement case was also well-known. Mr. Hanscomb has been accused of using this information to write a fictitious account to garner public sympathy and to sell papers. Kirby wants him silenced. Don't forget that it is more important now than ever before for Kirby to convince people you are dead."

"Why do ye say that, Elizabeth?"

"Because his lawsuit depends on it, as does every lie John Kirby ever told. You are the only one who can say Hamilton hurt you in Newgate. You are the only one who can say that poor old woman was murdered, and you are the only one who can prove Kirby attempted to illegally transport you. I must admit he has been quite convincing, has Kirby. Most people believe him, but Hawkesbury is not *most* people. He is a very intelligent man with a network of people throughout the country who feed him information. He relies on his own sources for news, not just what he reads in the papers."

"Baron Hawkesbury has far too much tact to say he thinks you are staying under our roof," Joseph Fry adds, "but he believes you are very much alive and that we know where you are."

My knees almost give out underneath me. "He kens I'm here?" Suddenly I feel the rough rope of the hangman's noose around my neck once more. "Please, Elizabeth, ye have to hide me!"

"It's fine, Libby," Elizabeth says with a reassuring voice. "Hawkesbury bears no love for John Kirby or Sir Cecil Hamilton, and while he may suspect you are a guest under my roof, he has no intention of seeing harm come to you. He has far bigger fish to fry, as they say."

I feel the air slowly return to my lungs. "Ye're certain of that?"

"More than certain." I hear Elizabeth's confidence in her words and start to feel better.

"So why was he here?" I ask.

"The words Sir Cecil and John Kirby are using are "libel" and "defamation." Do you know what they mean?"

"I cannae say I do." I've learned many new words since arriving in England, but these aren't amongst them.

"In short, they mean lying on purpose to damage a person's reputation," Joseph Fry explains. "Sir Cecil and John Kirby have started a lawsuit against Benjamin and the *Courier*. They have a court date set next week at the Court of King's Bench in Westminster.

"Why would they do such a thing?" I ask.

"To protect their position in society. You've told the world that a woman was murdered in Newgate by a turnkey, and that a peer of the realm bribed his way into the prison to attack a defenceless young girl. These are scandalous accusations, enough to bring both men down and so they are planning on destroying Mr. Hanscomb and the *Courier* in court."

"It's not right that they would threaten Mr. Hanscomb in such a way." I am infuriated that such evil men would try to ruin a fine reporter like Mr. Hanscomb for telling the truth.

"I agree completely," Elizabeth Fry says. "As does Baron Hawkesbury. That was why his secretary came today. He has invited you to appear at court to speak on behalf of Mr. Hanscomb. Your returning from the dead would make quite the scene!"

"What do you think I should do, Elizabeth?" Even though I want very much to help Mr. Hanscomb, I'm deathly afraid. The last time I ended up in a court, Sir Simon Le Blanc sentenced me to die.

"I think that you need to follow your conscience," says Elizabeth. "It is a most difficult task but much good could come from it."

"What would I have to say?"

"Just tell the truth, just as you did to Mr. Hanscomb. I believe your word could go a long way in having their lawsuit tossed out of court."

"When is this supposed to happen?" I ask.

"Today is Saturday. Lord Hawkesbury said that court meets at Westminster on Wednesday afternoon."

"Sir Cecil will be there, won't he? And Mr. Kirby?"

Elizabeth nods. "They will be."

I was scared before Elizabeth told me all this. Now I am terrified. "But you needn't worry about them. Baron Hawkesbury was very clear in his letter that *if* you were alive and *if* you agreed to speak to the court he would not give them any notice you were coming. Your presence would be a surprise. He also guaranteed your safety."

"He can do that?" After all that has happened to me, my faith in people in authority has been sorely tested.

Elizabeth does her best to reassure me. "Next to the Prime Minister himself, Baron Hawkesbury is the most powerful man in the country. If he says he can guarantee your safety, then he can."

I trust Elizabeth Fry and believe her. But more than that, I will not, cannot let this challenge to Mr. Hanscomb and the *Courier* go unanswered. It is my word as much as anything that is being questioned. Terrible things happened to my family and to me. I will not let anyone call them lies. "Please, Elizabeth, let this Baron Hawkesbury ken that I will go, and this court best be prepared to listen to some hard truths."

Chapter 35

IT IS A COLD DAY, the coldest of the year by far as Mrs. Fry's coach leaves Plashet House behind, the horses' hooves crunching on the snow, their breath steaming into the crisp air. "How are you feeling, Libby?" Elizabeth asks.

"Scared out of my wits." I've hardly slept in the days since agreeing to speak to the court, and despite Elizabeth's assurances to the contrary, the image of Sir Simon's gavel and the hangman's noose has flashed before my eyes more times than I care to think.

"I understand," Elizabeth says, "but I promise you that you will be safe. I will be there, and Lord Hawkesbury has assured me once more that no ill will come to you. Isn't that right, Joseph?"

"It is indeed." Joseph Fry has joined us as well, and I feel better knowing that such lovely people are willing to help me. I fall into a thoughtful silence, staring out the window as the carriage slowly rumbles along the cobblestones. I try to organize in my mind what I will say and how I will answer any questions the government men might ask of me.

Every few minutes the view of the passing streets disappears, the thin glass covered with the fog from my breath, and I must wipe it clean with my sleeve before it freezes over. We travel this way, Elizabeth knitting something or other, and myself deep in thought, staring out the window until the driver barks a short command to the two horses pulling the coach. The animals whinny as we stop. "That was a quicker trip than I'd thought," says Elizabeth as the driver steps down, opens the door and holds out his arm.

"Allow me, Ma'am," he says.

"I won't say no, not the condition I'm in these days," Elizabeth grins.

"You shouldn't have come, Elizabeth. Goodness knows that baby could arrive anytime now."

"I said as much as well," Joseph Fry says, "but as you can see, my wife is not one to listen to advice she doesn't want to hear."

"Don't be ridiculous, the both of you." Elizabeth steps cautiously to the ground with the assistance of the coachman.

"The doctor says I have another month at least, and most likely more, and even if I were in labour I'd still come. Can you imagine? Having the baby in Westminster, Joseph? Wouldn't that be something!"

Before Joseph Fry can answer, a well-dressed young man walks towards the coach. "It is my pleasure to see the both of you again," he says. Then he looks at me as I climb down from the coach. "And you must be the famous young Elizabeth. I have heard a great deal about you!"

"This is Mr. Walters, Baron Hawkesbury's private secretary," Elizabeth explains. "He is the man who came to our house earlier in the week."

I give the man my best curtsy. "'Tis a pleasure to meet ye."

"The pleasure is all mine. Baron Hawkesbury will be pleased as well to know you are right on time," says Mr. Walters. "Welcome to Westminster."

For the first time I take in my surroundings and am in awe at the grand building before me. "It looks like a palace," I say, staring up at the tall stone walls that tower into the sky.

"Westminster was indeed a palace at one time," Mr. Walters says as he leads us to a set of gilded wooden doors. The kings and queens of England used to live here until Henry VIII moved the royal residences to Whitehall Palace. Now? Westminster is home to the Court of King's Bench as well as the House of Commons and the House of Lords. This part of the palace is where the court meets."

Mr. Walters leans towards me and whispers. "I think a

couple of individuals in the room will be most surprised to see you, Mistress Scott. I'm feeling rather gleeful at the thought of it!" The hallway leads us to another large wooden door, this one beautifully decorated with carvings. "Are you ready?"

I draw in my breath to stop my teeth from chattering with fear. "As I'll ever be, Mr. Walters."

"You'll do very well, Libby," Elizabeth assures me. "You have the upper hand, so don't let Sir Cecil or John Kirby intimidate you. You have nothing to fear from them. Not any more."

"You'll do us all proud," Joseph Fry adds.

"Very well then," says Mr. Walters as he walks up the door. "Wait here, please. The proceeding has already started. I will go and fetch the Home Secretary."

Within a few seconds the door swings open and a very distinguished man steps out of the court. "I am indeed honoured to make your acquaintances," says Baron Hawkesbury. Hawkesbury is a tall man, dressed in a black suit, his hair light and thinning, his manners impeccable. He looks somehow familiar to me, but I can't place him. Still, I feel as if I've seen this man before.

Baron Hawkesbury shakes Joseph's hand first. "Mr. Fry, yours is a well-respected name in business. And you, Mrs. Fry," he adds bowing elegantly to Elizabeth. "As you know I am also aware of your concern over women in prison, and I admire you for it."

He takes my hand in his. "Young Elizabeth, your words in the *Courier* have made a most powerful impact on me. I am glad you are here. I am certain that you have some very important things to contribute to the proceedings and I am anxious to hear them, but before we enter, I must warn you that the room is quite full."

"For a lawsuit, my lord?" Joseph Fry seems surprised.

"Indeed. Usually something so mundane as a lawsuit would attract nobody save the parties involved and their barristers, if they even have any, but due to the publicity Mistress Scott's story in the *Courier* has generated, there is considerable excitement at the outcome."

Then Lord Hawkesbury turns to me. "You must be prepared for what you will see, young lady. "I think it is a fair thing to say that this lawsuit has attracted even more attention than your original trial!"

Chapter 36

THE COURTROOM IS SMALLER than I would have thought, with large wooden tables facing the judge's bench and rich oak panelling and portraits of lawyers and judges lining the walls. The gallery is full of padded leather seats, all occupied with men, while at the bench sits a robed and wigged judge. Two barristers stand before him likewise and wearing powdered wigs upon their heads. Mr. Hanscomb sits in the dock before the judge and his face breaks out in surprise when he sees me.

Baron Hawkesbury addresses the chamber. "Forgive the interruption, but may I present to the court, Mr. and Mrs. Joseph Fry and Elizabeth Scott. Mistress Scott has volunteered to speak on behalf of Mr. Benjamin Hanscomb and the London *Courier* in the matter before the courts. It is her story after all that has resulted in this lawsuit."

The courtroom erupts. "You said she was dead!" Sir Cecil Hamilton stares at me as if he is seeing a ghost before he turns his gaze to John Kirby, the Keeper of Newgate Prison, who looks at this moment as if he's been sucking on a lemon.

"You most certainly did," says the judge, his eyes darting between me and John Kirby. You produced a death certificate in her name. Explain yourself, sir."

"Your honour, I thought she had died of disease in the prison," Kirby says smoothly, not missing a beat. "Both the foreman of my guards and the prison doctor confirmed it. It's not as if I lay eyes on every prisoner who dies, after all."

"And yet here she is, alive and breathing," says the judge suspiciously. "How do you account for that, sir?"

"I fully intend to find that out for myself," Kirby says. "It sounds like somebody with an agenda managed to bribe my staff. I shall launch a full inquiry upon my return to Newgate."

"It would seem that you have underestimated this plucky young girl's resolve," Hawkesbury says. "To survive both your lies and your attempts to silence her."

"She's no girl! She is a liar and a fugitive from justice and I demand she be returned to my custody!" If John Kirby was startled to see me standing before him, he has quickly managed to shake it off.

"Gaol be damned!" Hamilton looks at me as if I were a murderer. "She needs to swing from the gibbet! Home Secretary or no, you've stuck your nose into my affairs once too often, my lord."

"Neither of those things will happen," Hawkesbury says. "Civil litigation falls under my position, and Mistress Scott is here by my invitation to testify. Once she has spoken she will leave this place a free girl. Somebody wanted her silenced and I have my suspicions that *that somebody* is in this court today."

The court explodes once again. Half a dozen men, writers like Mr. Hanscomb, judging by the way they scratch their pens across their notebooks, hang on to the Home Secretary's every word.

"Order in this court, gentlemen, order!" the judge says firmly. "I shall not have this hearing turn into a farce."

Both Hamilton and Kirby look as if they are about to reply, but a steely glance from the judge silences them as Hawkesbury ushers me toward the front. "My apologies, your honour," the Home Secretary says. "I would beg your forgiveness for surprising the court with Elizabeth Scott's appearance, but I feel it important she speak since she is the only one who can corroborate Mr. Hanscomb's story."

"She is a liar," shouts Hamilton. "She has no place here."

The judge is having none of Sir Cecil's outburst. "You will watch your tongue, sir. Lord or not, this is my courtroom and you shall act in a civil manner. I shall recess while I consider this rather unorthodox request from a most unexpected witness. Mr. Hanscomb, you may remove yourself from the dock. We will continue with your testimony if needed when the court reconvenes."

"All rise!" says a bailiff as the judge excuses himself. Those in attendance stand quietly until the judge has left. Once the door shuts, however, the room erupts in chatter once more.

"Now that we have a moment, Mistress Scott, allow me to introduce to you some members of Parliament who have been following your story with substantial interest," says Hawkesbury. "This is Lord Fitzroy, Member of Parliament for Bury St. Edmunds."

The youngest man at the table, slim and handsome, stands up and bows to me as if I were a queen. "A great pleasure, Mistress Scott. I was particularly moved by your account."

Next to him is an older man, shorter and rounder with short white hair. "Good afternoon, young lady," he says politely. "My name is Reginald Pole Carew, Member for Fowey. Like my colleague, Lord Fitzroy, I am an admirer of yours."

"Mr. Pole Carew is being modest," Hawkesbury says. "He is more than just a Member of Parliament. He is the former Undersecretary of State for the Home Department and is currently a member of the Privy Council. He is most highly thought of in this House, as is Mr. Thomas Babington, Member of Parliament for Leicester."

The man next to Mr. Pole Carew, slight and balding, stands

up and bows as well. "A great honour to meet you, Mistress Scott."

"I cannot agree more." The last man in the room, the oldest by the look of him, walks over and shakes my hand. "Thomas Coke, Member of Parliament for Derby. It is my privilege to meet the girl behind such powerful words."

"'Tis my pleasure to meet all of ye as well." I am taken aback by the manners and courtesy these gentlemen have extended me. My only experience with noblemen to this point has been with Sir Cecil Hamilton who, sitting there with a bitter look on his face, now looks anything but noble.

"Now it is Mr. Coke who is being modest," says Hawkesbury. "He is renowned in both this House and across the country for his work in agriculture, his tolerance for all and his support of the common Englishman."

"Renowned?" Apparently, the praise heaped upon Mr. Coke does not sit well with Sir Cecil who overhears our conversation. "He supported the Americans in their blasted revolution and sympathized with the Catholics and the French revolutionaries as well. The lot of you are a disgrace to this country and your names! You're all busybodies, abolitionists, reformers, and sympathizers of the criminal class! None of you have any business being here today."

Hawkesbury looked about to say something when Coke cut him off with an easy wave of his hand. "Come now, Cecil, not all of us can be robber barons or heartless industrialists. We must find our opportunities where we can. Besides, the courts are open to all, and I would wager the girl has some interesting things to say about you. Don't you want to hear about them?"

The others laugh heartily at the reply, a response that does not sit well with Sir Cecil, judging by the deep shade of red spreading across his face. Despite my initial fear of the man, I find myself grinning as well.

"Libby!" Mr. Hanscomb hurries over to me. "What on earth are you doing here?"

"When I heard you were in trouble because of my story, I knew I had to speak on yer behalf."

"There is no need, Libby, though I must admit I was glad to see you. Sir Cecil's barrister was making me most uncomfortable before you arrived."

"What else would you expect from Mr. Corbett?" The man speaking to me now is the other barrister, a young fellow who looks slightly uncomfortable in his wig and robes. "Corbett's earned the name 'the Bloodhound' for good reason, and not just because of the way he looks."

I see what the lawyer means. Mr. Corbett, currently huddled at the table with Sir Cecil and John Kirby, is a big man with watery eyes and large jowls. "Corbett's relentless. Once the Bloodhound starts with a witness, he doesn't stop until he's won his point. I've seen people break down in the box and weep because of him."

"You know I'm in trouble when the barrister retained by the *Courier* for my defence is an admirer of his opponent," says Mr. Hanscomb, a wry look on his face.

"Philip Dutton," the young lawyer says, shaking my hand. "I wouldn't say I am an admirer of the Bloodhound, but I am certainly cautious of him. And for good reason."

Sir Cecil Hamilton lifts his impressive bulk out of his chair and waddles over to us. "I don't know what you're trying to prove with this ridiculous sideshow, Hawkesbury," he says. "This insidious little wretch is a liar and a criminal and she deserves to hang."

"The girl claims you came into her cell and beat her within an inch of her life, Hamilton", says Lord Fitzroy. "What do you say to such a heinous crime?"

"I say it's a filthy lie and that I will . . ." before Hamilton can finish the threat, a hush sweeps through the court. "All rise!" the bailiff says as the door to the judge's chambers open, "The court is now in session. The honourable Justice Martin Graham presiding!"

"A part of me hopes the judge does allow you to speak, girl," Hamilton whispers before taking his seat. "Corbett will tear you apart. And when he is finished with you, you'll wish you really did die in Newgate."

Chapter 37

"COUNSEL, APPROACH THE BENCH," Judge Graham orders. At the command, both Mr. Corbett and Mr. Dutton hurry to the judge, who leans down towards them, speaking so softly I cannot hear a word. The whole court is hushed, everyone in the room straining to hear what is going on.

After a few moments, both nod. Mr. Dutton hurries over to Mr. Hanscomb and myself, face flushed. "His honour is going to let Elizabeth Scott testify."

"Are you certain, Libby?" Hanscomb looks very worried. "The Bloodhound is merciless. It isn't an idle threat Hamilton made; take it from me."

No doubt he is. My first experience in an English court was at the Old Bailey. I was shown no mercy there, why would I expect it here? "I'm ready, Mr. Hanscomb. It's my honour at stake as well. After all I've been through, I've got naught to fear from the likes of him."

"Mr. Hanscomb, you are excused for now. Elizabeth Scott, approach." I hear excited whispers behind me as I walk towards the dock. "You are prepared to give testimony to the court?" Judge Graham seems stern and serious, but unlike Sir Simon Le Blanc I sense no cruelty in his voice as he speaks to me.

"Aye, my laird. I am."

Very well. Bailiff please swear the witness in and we shall begin."

I raise my hand, take an oath promising to speak nothing but the truth, then I sit down. "Mr. Dutton. Your witness." Judge Graham says.

"Elizabeth Scott," he begins. "Would you please begin by telling the court how you ended up in Newgate Prison?"

For the next twenty minutes I speak. Mr. Dutton does not interrupt and the entire court listens in silence. As I give my testimony, the Bloodhound sits between John Kirby and Sir Cecil. He takes notes as both whisper into his ears.

"Thank you, Mistress Scott," Mr. Dutton says. "If you could now go into some detail about the incident between yourself and Sir Cecil Hamilton that occurred inside your cell."

"*Alleged* incident," says the Bloodhound. "My client vehemently denies such an encounter ever occurred."

"Apologies, my learned friend," says Mr. Dutton. He turns

to me. "Elizabeth Scott, can you speak about the *alleged* incident?"

"There is naught alleged about it," I say before recounting the horrible events. As I speak, I hear oohs and ahs from the court.

"Thank you, Mistress Scott," Mr. Dutton says again. "Now if you could tell the court about the murder of the prisoner known as Dorothy."

"*Alleged* murder," barks the Bloodhound.

"A brute of a man, a turnkey named Alfred Hobbes, killed her," I begin. Once again, the court listens intently, the silence broken only by gasps of outrage.

When I am finished, Dutton addresses the judge. "Your honour, this brave young girl has corroborated the *Courier*'s story word for word. She spoke the truth and has more than proved that this spurious lawsuit needs to be dismissed immediately. More than that, it is apparent to me that the authorities need to pursue criminal charges against both John Kirby and Sir Cecil Hamilton, as well as the murderer Alfred Hobbes. One or both of these men conspired to have Libby Scott silenced and they must be held to account."

"Your opinion is noted by the court," Judge Graham says. "Mr. Corbett, do you have any questions of this witness?"

The Bloodhound stands up, smooths down his robe and approaches. "I do indeed, your honour. "This shan't take long."

The lawyer for Sir Cecil and John Kirby takes a moment to collect his thoughts then begins to speak. "Elizabeth Scott, you blame Sir Cecil for the deaths of your parents and that of your brother, do you not?"

"Aye, and a hundred other poor innocent souls. 'Tis at his factory they died, and if it weren't for him Duncan would never have got on that ship in Liverpool." I swore to speak the truth and so I have. No doubt everyone in the court thinks I meant the *Leopard*, not the *Sylph*, and I hope that my omission doesn't count as lying.

The barrister nods knowingly. "And you blame him for your subsequent incarceration, do you not?"

I feel my anger rise as I look at Sir Cecil, sitting there beside John Kirby, a smug smile on his face. "Aye, of course. Most of the misery in my life is because of that man. And because of Mr. Kirby as well," I add.

"So, you are telling me that you seek vengeance against these two gentlemen?"

"That isn't what I said! I want justice fer my family and fer Dorothy certainly. But justice is not the same as vengeance."

"*Justice?*" the man's voice drops and his eyes narrow. "You seek *justice*? For what, exactly? You lost your family in a terrible mill fire. That much is true, but did Sir Cecil light the match that burned the factory down?"

"Of course not, but . . ."

"And did Sir Cecil force your brother to assault him?"

"Nae, but that's not what happened. Sir Cecil . . . ."

"And did Sir Cecil force your brother to board that ill-fated ship?"

I am suddenly very flustered by the questions. "I dinnae ken what ye are trying to say, my laird."

"What I'm trying to say, *girl*, is that while unfortunate things have happened to you, no doubt, Sir Cecil did not cause them. In fact, Sir Cecil Hamilton is the real victim in this court; he and Mr. Kirby as well, men of standing in our country, men who have had their reputations slurred by your vile lies. They are the ones who need justice."

I cannot believe what I am hearing. "They are the victims?"

The Bloodhound's voice changes, a hard edge replacing the gentle tone. "When his mill burned down, Sir Cecil lost untold thousands of pounds. When your brute of a brother attacked him he near lost his life, and when you accused him of attacking you in your well-earned cell in Newgate, your slanderous words caused irreparable harm to his honour. I also have little doubt that someone in this courtroom ordered the girl transported and that the Home Secretary had a hand in it."

Mr. Dutton leaps up, his face red and flustered. "Your honour! Please! I insist this badgering and these utterly ridiculous allegations stop immediately!"

Corbett presses on. "Tell me, Mistress Scott, what day did this *alleged* assault occur? And, for good measure what day did the *alleged* murder of the old woman happen? Let us deal with both of your lies once and for all."

"I, I dinnae ken fer sure."

"And what time of day did this *alleged* assault and this *alleged* murder occur?"

"'Tis hard to keep track of time when a person is locked away. I cannae say fer sure."

"And who witnessed this *alleged* assault and this *alleged* murder?" he asks, hammering away at me.

"Hobbes, the turnkey," I reply. "He was there. He saw. He killed Dorothy." Finally, I am given a question I can answer.

"Perhaps you could ask this Hobbes to testify, your honour," Mr. Dutton suggests. "And then send him back to his own prison in chains while he awaits a trial at the Old Bailey for murder."

"You read my mind, Mr. Dutton," Judge Graham replies. "Mr. Kirby. Your gaoler, Alfred Hobbes by name. I would talk to him. We can have a carriage readied immediately to bring him here. I would like to hear what he has to say about all of this."

At the mention of Hobbes' name, John Kirby's face breaks into a sly smile. "I'm afraid that won't be possible, your honour. Mr. Hobbes has, unfortunately, recently passed away. He picked up a sickness from the prison just before the Scott girl was sent to the transport ship. He didn't survive it."

"Am I to believe that the one person who can testify to both of this young woman's claims is dead?" the judge says suspiciously.

I don't know what to think of this shocking news. Hobbes was a brute, but strangely the thought of him dead brings me no peace.

Mr. Dutton speaks up immediately. "Your honour! Apart

from the say-so of John Kirby, what evidence is there the turnkey is dead? This is far too convenient!"

"Tragic, not convenient, your honour," the Bloodhound says, taking a piece of paper from his files. "Mr. Hobbes was a valued employee, good at his job by all accounts. He will be sorely missed in Newgate. As for evidence? I present to you his death certificate."

The Bloodhound lays down the paper in front of the judge who reads it carefully before passing it over to Mr. Dutton. "On this account Mr. Kirby can validate the death. He saw Hobbes' body with his own eyes, did you not?"

"Indeed I did," Kirby says. "He was a loyal employee. He shall be missed."

Cholera. It seems genuine enough," the judge says. "It would appear that if Mr. Alfred Hobbes is to be judged for his actions, it will be by a higher authority than I."

"Well spoken, your honour," the Bloodhound says. "And without any witness to corroborate the girl's falsehoods, I feel I must insist that this lawsuit be settled in our favour immediately. We are talking about the word of a peer of the realm against that of a member of the criminal class. Surely the courts cannot deny my clients justice."

"My laird, there is another witness to Mad Dorothy's death," I say quickly. "Polly Snell, a prisoner like me. She saw it happen plain as day."

"Is there an inmate at Newgate by that name, Mr. Kirby?" asks Judge Graham. "I would have her testify."

Once again, a greasy smile breaks out on Kirby's face. "Indeed, there *was* a prisoner by that name, but she recently had her sentence for theft commuted and has since been recently released. London is a vast city; I have no idea where she would be."

"Your honour!" Mr. Dutton simply cannot believe what he is hearing. Nor can I for that matter.

The Bloodhound takes two other sheets of paper from his files and gives one to the judge. "No doubt my learned friend wants proof. May it please the court to examine Mistress Snell's record of release."

Once again both Judge Graham and Mr. Dutton peer closely at the offered paper. "Freed three weeks ago. Do you have any idea where this Mistress Snell may be living?" the judge asks me.

"Nae, my laird." Even if I did, Polly was the one who reported me to Kirby for telling Elizabeth Fry about Dorothy's death. She would not be of any help to me.

The Bloodhound deposits the other piece of paper in front of the judge. "There was indeed a prisoner known as Mad Dorothy at Newgate, but she died of a fall. It was an accident, and certainly not murder." With a dramatic wave of his hand, the Bloodhound lays the paper down in front of the judge. "Here is her death certificate."

"That is nae true!" I cry. "Hobbes struck her with a gin bottle! I saw it with my own eyes!"

I feel utterly helpless. I look in desperation at Mr. Dutton, but I see nothing but resignation on his face. He knows all is lost. No doubt Elizabeth and Joseph Fry do as well, judging by the sad expressions on their faces. Mr. Hanscomb looks ill, and even Baron Hawkesbury and the other Members of Parliament seem defeated.

"It would seem that there are no witnesses to corroborate the story in the *Courier*," Judge Graham begins. As he speaks, I turn my head to Sir Cecil Hamilton and John Kirby. Both of those horrible men look positively gleeful, Hamilton returns my gaze and looks at me, the same odd smile he gave me just before he entered my cell.

Suddenly I am back there, locked away, cowering against the wall, watching Hamilton approach. I smell his breath, feel his presence, see his hammy fist about to strike me, one awful image after the other, flashing like lightning bolts in my brain,

"And so I deem that this lawsuit be settled in favour of . . ."

"Wait my laird!" I almost shout the words as I interrupt the judge. "Sir Cecil was in my cell at Newgate and I can prove it!"

Chapter 38

"YOU CAN PROVE NOTHING because everything you say is a fabrication. As I said earlier, your honour, who in their right mind would believe a criminal over a peer of the realm? Despite the Home Secretary's assurances, I also ask that once you settle this suit in our favour, you should send this wretch back to Newgate immediately."

The Bloodhound sounds confident, but as I look at Sir Cecil I can see the shadow of uncertainty on his face. He is leaning forward, listening intently to what I am about to say. Beside him Kirby looks confused. A shiver goes through my body at the thought of returning to Newgate. Hobbes is dead, and I have no doubt Sir Cecil and John Kirby are responsible for it. And Polly? Was she killed as well and the release paper a clever lie? I do not doubt it was. The lengths these men will go to in order to save themselves are staggering.

"How, young lady? How can you prove such a thing?" asks Judge Graham, and I swear I hear hope in his voice.

"Sir Cecil has a ring on the small finger of his right hand. I saw it before he hurt me, clear as a bell. It glittered in the lantern light. It is a golden ring, the image of an oak tree is carved into it, surrounded by red stones." I run my hand over my scarred cheek. "It cut me. I still bear the mark from it."

"Utterly ridiculous," Hamilton says, though I notice his hands are now tucked under the table.

"The only way the girl could know such a thing is if you were there, Sir Cecil," Mr. Dutton says, seizing the opportunity. "Your honour, please, make him show the court his hand."

"I will do no such thing! "Hamilton protests. "She's the one in the dock not me! The wretch is lying! I am a member of the House of Lords and I will not answer to a common Highland criminal!"

"Oh, I think you will, Cecil." The voice is a new one, coming from the door behind me.

"Mr. Prime Minister!" Judge Graham says, quickly standing.

"Your Grace," says Baron Hawkesbury, bowing as an old man, a powdered wig on his head, walks into the room. Everyone else at the table, even Kirby and Hamilton, stand up as William Cavendish-Bentinck, the 3rd Duke of Portland and Prime Minister of the United Kingdom, approaches.

"The oak tree figures prominently on your family crest does it not, Hamilton?" the Prime Minister asks.

"Yes, your grace," Hamilton reluctantly responds.

"Then I would see that ring, Sir Cecil. Approach," the judge orders.

"I must object!" says the Bloodhound.

"Objection noted," replied the judge. "Sir Cecil, the court is waiting for you."

Slowly and reluctantly, Hamilton climbs out of his chair, his face red with rage. He waddles towards the judge, scowling at me the entire time. "The ring, sir," asks the judge. "Give it to me."

Sure enough, I see the familiar gold ring on Hamilton's finger. "Your honour, I protest! This is ludicrous!" The Bloodhound tries once more to prevent the judge from seeing the ring.

Judge Graham is having none of it. "Another word from either one of you and I'll hold you in contempt," he warns Hamilton and the Bloodhound. "The ring, Sir Cecil. Now."

"Damn you, girl," Hamilton says as he slowly twists the ring off his finger. With one last angry pull, Hamilton spins the ring from his finger and slams it heavily down in front of Judge Graham.

"Thank you," says the judge. "You will get your ring back in a moment, but for now return to your seat."

Hamilton does as asked, his face a black cloud of rage as he sits down. "Approach, Mistress Scott," the judge says gently. "Are you familiar with a fairy tale called *Cinderella*?"

"Aye, my laird," I say when I am standing before him.

"The glass slipper fit that young lady," he says, leaning down toward my face, Hamilton's ring in hand. "Let us see if this ring matches your wound."

I wince as the cool gem touches my skin, right on top of the scar. "Mr. Corbett, Mr. Dutton, approach."

"Coincidence," Corbett says, though there is no conviction in his voice.

"The ring matches the injury to her face perfectly!" Mr. Dutton says excitedly, the courtroom erupting in cheers. "Our Scottish Cinderella is telling the truth!"

"I should have killed you that day!" Hamilton spits.

"What did you say?" The judge turns sharply to Sir Cecil.

"He said nothing, your honour," the Bloodhound replies, but it is too late.

"He admitted to being there!" cries Mr. Dutton. "Everyone heard it."

"Perhaps not everyone but I most certainly did," the judge says. "Sir Cecil, you have perjured yourself in this courtroom. Your entire testimony is worthless." He bangs his gavel. "This lawsuit is hereby tossed out. Mr. Hanscomb, Mistress Scott, you are free to go."

The Prime Minister walks up to me, and gently runs his hand over the scar on my face. "And rightly so. A right dastardly deed on your part, Hamilton," he says. "Reprehensible. And as for you, Mr. Kirby, I have no doubt of the role you played in this sorry affair. I am sure a thorough investigation will reveal the truth behind this girl's illegal transportation, the death of the old woman, and other crimes as well, no doubt. You were right to intervene in her case and spare her from the gallows, Hawkesbury."

"My laird? I'm alive because of ye?" It is then I realize where I'd seen Baron Hawkesbury before. "Ye were the man standing beside Kirby when I stood upon the gallows, weren't you? It was ye who saved my life!"

"Yes, but it was because of Mrs. Fry, if truth be told. She wrote a most compelling letter. I investigated the matter and told Sir Simon Le Blanc that commuting your sentence was in the country's best interest, but I had to look at you to be certain. When I saw you, there was no doubt in my mind you were innocent. Besides, your death could have caused significant unrest in the Kingdom, particularly in Scotland."

I look at Hawkesbury with gratitude. "I cannae thank you enough, my laird."

"I must say there were many who disagreed with me," he says, "but you have more than justified my decision. Your testimony has proven that we have much work to do in this country to improve the lot of the poor and working class."

The Prime Minister looks at me with kind eyes. "I am sorry for all that has befallen you, young lady," he says. "I have likewise read your account in the *Courier*. I had hoped it was not true; I did not want to believe that men of such stature could be so dastardly, but I can see now it is. I believe you, as will the rest of the United Kingdom."

"Thank ye, my laird" I curtsy to the Prime Minister, my heart swelling at his words.

"No, Mistress Scott. Thank you. Rest assured that no further harm will come to you or the paper that told your story. You have been most brave in the face of adversity and both myself and the country owe you a debt for your courage. Believe me when I say that you will finally receive the justice you have been denied so long."

Chapter 39

THIS IS ALL BECAUSE of you, Libby," Elizabeth Fry says. A month has passed since I testified and much has happened since. "Baron Hawkesbury has ordered a formal commission on prison reform, John Kirby has been dismissed from Newgate, and Sir Cecil has been publicly humiliated."

"Humiliation is hardly fair payment for all the things he's done to me and my family," I say.

"I understand how you can feel that way, but the government has taken away multiple contracts from his factories. He won't go to jail, but he has lost thousands and thousands of pounds and his reputation. It is a start."

Elizabeth is right, no doubt. Formal commission aside, the

rich and the powerful in England are not likely to face the same punishment for their crimes as regular people. "At least ye have been given an important role, Elizabeth."

Of all the outcomes of my words, the one that pleases me the most is the position Lord Hawkesbury has given Elizabeth. She has been asked to formally work with the female and child prisoners at Newgate and the other English prisons. She has been tasked to teach them to read and write so that when they are released from prison they have opportunities to find meaningful work and a good life.

"And now we need to find something for you as well," Elizabeth says. "It's high time you move on with your life and I think I may have just the thing."

"What do ye have in mind," I ask. My future is something the two of us have been talking about for weeks.

"As you know, our family are bankers," she says. One of Joseph's cousins in particular is doing quite well. Have you heard of Bristol?"

"Nae, Elizabeth. Why?" I ask.

Elizabeth replies with a smile. "It is a small city to the west where they live. He has a wife and two young children, and they are looking for a teacher for their children. I suggested to our cousin that you would be a tremendous governess and he agreed. Despite what Lord Hawkesbury says, I don't trust Sir Cecil. You have caused him great humiliation and financial loss, and I fear he may want vengeance. After all, he's done it before. Bristol is a very long way from here and you will be safe from Sir Cecil."

Bristol. I don't know where Bristol is, but I like the thought that I will have a useful job and be far away from London. Sir Cecil aside, this city is too big, too busy, for a girl raised in the Highlands. But there is something else keeps me from leaping at the opportunity, something that has been greatly on my mind of late. Should by some miracle Duncan return, he will no doubt hear about what has happened to me. He will learn about my adventures and he will come looking for me, I just know it.

"Libby? What is it?" Elizabeth Fry asks me. "You look like you are half a world away."

"Nae, Elizabeth, I'm here in London, but someone I care about is on the other side of the world. I need to talk to ye about Duncan."

"Oh Libby," Mrs. Fry says gently. "I know it's hard, but you have to find a way to let him go. Your brother's dead. He drowned in the Atlantic.

I take a deep breath, about to share my deepest secret. "Nae, Elizabeth. He isn't."

Chapter 40

THE MONTHS GO BY quickly in Bristol. Mrs. Fry and her family are kind, the children I teach lovely, and I have my very own room in their house overlooking the garden. I receive letters from Elizabeth every month or so, but I hear nothing about my brother, and as months pass one after the other, I lose hope I will ever see Duncan again. Sometimes I even go weeks now without thinking of him.

Still, I'm comfortable and not unhappy, and am at peace that this is how my life will be until a warm day in late September when I volunteer to go on a trip to the market. Usually Mrs. Cavanaugh, Mrs. Fry's housekeeper, does the shopping, but it is such a lovely day, I leap at the chance to go to the market.

I am almost ready to leave when we hear a loud, unexpected knock on the door. Mrs. Cavanaugh peers through the eyehole out onto the threshold of the door. "Two men. I don't know them," she whispers. "Quickly girl, step into the pantry."

Although many months have passed since the trial, Mrs. Cavanaugh has been charged with keeping an eye out for me, and it is a task she takes most seriously. I follow her command and run quickly to the pantry, our small storage room by the kitchen.

When I am safely in the pantry, Mrs. Cavanaugh opens the door. "Yes?" she says. I hold the pantry door open a crack to listen. I can't see anything, but I can hear well enough from my hiding place.

"Hello," a man says with a Highland lilt. "I'm looking for someone. A Scottish lass, Elizabeth Scott. Do ye ken her?"

Somehow, I manage to keep my wits about me at the mention of my name. At first, I fear the men have been sent by Sir Cecil, that he has found me, and they are here to take his revenge upon me. "This is the Fry residence, is it not?" the man asks.

"What is it to you? Mrs. Cavanaugh demands.

"'Tis everything to me. I've been looking fer my sister fer years. She's supposed to be here. Mrs. Fry said so herself, back in London. I need to see her."

I feel the air rush from my lungs as the man speaks, but I dare not believe it can be Duncan. Most likely it is an agent of Sir Cecil who is trying to find me, lying to convince me to show my face. It cannot be my brother, not after all this time.

Mrs. Cavanaugh is having none of it. "I'm sorry but I've never heard of anyone named Elizabeth Scott."

"Not here? Libby's not here? Why would Elizabeth Fry have told such a cruel lie to me, Bill?"

"Hold on a minute, Trap," the other man says. His name is Bill by the sounds of things.

"Aye?"

Trap. He said the name Trap. It cannot be Duncan.

"Think about it," the man named Bill says. "The Mrs. Fry woman said your sister made quite the name for herself. She will be in hiding because of it, right?"

"Good day to you, sirs." I hear Mrs. Cavanaugh say. "You must leave now, or I'll call the authorities!"

"This woman doesn't know us from Adam. Do you really think she'd admit to housing a fugitive to a couple of strangers?"

Nae, I dinnae think she would."

"That Mrs. Fry woman told the truth about everything else, right down to the nameplate on the door. Why would she lie about Libby? Besides, she's nearly a saint, she is, according to everyone in London. Lying ain't something a person like that would do, seems to me."

"I insist you leave at once!" Mrs. Cavanaugh orders. I stand frozen in place, unable to move.

"You've travelled across the world and back, Trap. What harm is there in taking a few more steps?"

The one called Trap agrees. "I'm sorry about this, Ma'am, but I cannae leave here without knowing fer sure."

Suddenly I hear a loud noise as the men push their way past Mrs. Cavanaugh and into the house. "Libby! Libby Scott! Are ye here?"

"Libby Scott! I'm with your brother, Duncan! Can you hear me?"

"Leave this house immediately!" cries Mrs. Cavanaugh. "This is shocking! I must protest!"

The men ignore her. "Libby!" the one who claims to be my brother shouts as he enters the kitchen. He is now only two feet from where I'm hidden. "Please, fer guidness sake if yer here, answer!"

I slowly open the pantry door. The men have their backs to me, but I can see that they are young. They are dressed like sailors and wear their hair long. One even has a wooden leg.

"Who did ye say ye were looking fer?" They spin on their heels at the sound of my voice. The one with the wooden leg is a stranger to me, but there is something very familiar about the other. He has long blonde hair and blue eyes.

Eyes I've seen before.

"I thought I told you to stay hidden," Mrs. Cavanaugh says though I barely hear her.

"Do I ken ye, stranger?" I ask, voice shaking but I know the answer to the question. I know this young man very well. "Duncan?" I feel the tears well up in my eyes.

"Aye, Libby," my brother says as he embraces me. "It most certainly is."

Chapter 41

"I CANNOT TELL YOU how sorry I am, Duncan," says Elizabeth Fry. It is a warm, late-September day. Autumn asters and crocus bloom purple and red in the walled back-garden of the Fry house in Bristol as I drink tea with my brother, his friend Bill and Elizabeth Fry.

"I had to leave London and come to the Bristol house myself to make sure all was in order," she explains. "I was so excited to see Duncan that I completely forgot to write him a letter of introduction. You were lucky, young man, to make your way past Mrs. Cavanaugh. She is very fond of Libby and quite protective."

"You were at that, young man," Mrs. Cavanaugh says, pouring fresh tea. Mrs. Cavanaugh had done her very best to keep Duncan and Bill out of the house, and I am glad to say that she failed.

"Never mind all that," says Duncan. "We're together now and safe at last."

"Together, perhaps, but not quite safe," Elizabeth Fry reminds us. "Libby cannot be safe as long as she is in England. She put her life at risk after all, and some corrupt rich and powerful men were brought to justice because of her. These are men with long memories and even longer reaches."

"Aye," I say. "'Tis a shame. I quite like Bristol, but I ken I cannae stay here."

"It is to that end I came," says Elizabeth. "Apart from making sure you found each other, of course." Elizabeth reaches into a small leather satchel she has with her and removes a leather pouch.

"This came for you just after Duncan left London," she says to me.

"What is it?" Who on earth in London would give me mail, let alone a large, strange-looking bag.

"Payment for what you did," Mrs. Fry explains. "Your story sold a great many papers. I ensured that you would get a percentage of that for your great bravery in Newgate and when you testified in court."

I gasp when I open the pouch. "'Tis a fortune!" I exclaim, staring shocked at the pile of gold and silver coins. This money must be the result of the deal she had struck with the *Courier*.

"Not quite a fortune and certainly less than she deserves

for what she did, but enough to allow a certain brother and sister I know to get out of England and start a brand-new life wherever they may fancy."

I hold the bag of coins tight to my chest. "So where shall we go, Duncan? Scotland? Malta? You said it was nice there."

"I think I ken a place," Duncan says. "Perhaps it's time we finally sailed across the Atlantic together, Libby."

"Montreal? Though I'm not certain I want to travel as far west as ye went."

"Aye, Montreal or near abouts is fine for me," Duncan replies.

I turn to Bill. In the short time they have been with me at the Fry houshold, I've heard about their adventures at sea and know that Duncan and Bill are the best of friends. "There's money enough for three to travel."

"I couldn't impose," Bill replies.

"Impose? Don't be ridiculous, Bill! You saved my brother's life on the *Cerberus*! It's the least I could do."

"Actually 'twas me who saved his life," Duncan says with a grin.

"In that case I say yes!" Bill laughs.

"So what do we do now, Duncan?" I ask. "You're the world traveller, after all."

Before he can say anything, Elizabeth speaks up. "Somehow, I had a feeling you'd consider going back to Montreal," she says.

"As you know, my husband's family are chocolate merchants. They sell their wares across Europe and across the Atlantic to Canada and the United States. It just so happens we have a rather large delivery of chocolate scheduled to sail next week on the *Walrus* from Bristol to Quebec City. The captain is a friend of my family. He said there's room enough on board for two."

"Elizabeth grins at Bill. "Though I'm certain he can squeeze in another."

"Elizabeth!" I hug my friend at her offer, as does Duncan.

"So what do we do now?" Duncan asks, repeating my question. "We pack what few things we have and then use a few of yer coins to get some guid winter coats. Believe me, it gets colder in Montreal than ye can possibly imagine!"

ABOUT THE AUTHOR

David Starr is a prize-winning author of three previous novels published by Ronsdale Press. *The Nor'Wester* (2017) and *The King's Shilling* (2018) are young adult novels which tell the story of Libby and Duncan of which *The Girl of Newgate Prison* is the sequel. *Like Joyful Tears* (2019) is an adult novel about the horrendous events during the civil war in South Sudan. He has also published another three books by other publishers. In *Bombs to Books*, he chronicled the stories of refugee children and their families coming to B.C. *Golden Goal* is a young adult soccer-themed book for reluctant readers. *The Insider's Guide to K–12 Education in B.C.* is a resource guide for parents about the B.C. school system. David grew up in Fort St. James, a town that plays a large role in *The Nor'Wester*. He now lives in greater Vancouver with his wife, four children and a dog named Buster. He combines the roles of high school principal and author. Please visit him at www.davidjstarr.org.

MARQUIS

Québec, Canada